THE
DARK
EXISTENCE

Lydia Becker

THE SILVER SPARROW

Copyright © 2022 The Silver Sparrow
All rights reserved
First Edition

NEWMAN SPRINGS PUBLISHING
320 Broad Street
Red Bank, NJ 07701

First originally published by Newman Springs Publishing 2022

ISBN 978-1-63881-797-0 (Paperback)
ISBN 978-1-63881-798-7 (Digital)

Printed in the United States of America

To all the dreamers with a story in their hearts.

JASON

Fear. I remember feeling fear. My heart raced, my palms were sweating, and I did everything I could to take slow, easy breaths. I wanted to leave, but I didn't want my fear to show. It would only make things worse.

He stood at the head of the class, answering a question on the blackboard. I remember how every girl in the class swooned over him. Maybe it was the flawless face almost hidden by his raven-black hair or the lanky build that also carried a presence of strength and confidence, or maybe it was the piercing gaze of his auburn eyes.

I watched him as he turned to the class and repeated the answer, but I wasn't really listening. That gaze haunted me. It held a dark and mysterious air that intrigued or intimidated anyone who met him. It was only more obvious when he rarely spoke to anyone and kept mostly to himself.

My blood ran cold as he walked by, passing me in the row. I stared at my book in front of me as he walked to his desk three rows down behind me. I didn't dare look back. I could easily feel his eyes like lasers on the back of my neck. My thoughts swam with questions as I sat there.

Why me? Why did this have to happen to me? Of all the people in the world! Of all the guys in my school! Why on earth did it have to happen to me?

I was even beginning to be afraid of the dark, always feeling like he would be right there waiting for me. After all, he did try to kill me.

That night floated back into my mind for about the hundredth time since it happened. It had been five nights ago—the most terrifying night of my life.

*****

The silence of the night was cut by the groaning of the heavy doors as we walked into the empty front hall. My companion laughed as he walked in, his wide build causing the floor to creak. "Don't be a wuss. It's just a stupid house."

It was a very abandoned house, one we should never have been in. I could see the little moonlight that came in through the boarded windows reflecting off his red hair, and his blue eyes stood out in the dark. Benji Banks, possibly my greatest mistake.

I followed silently, being a good bit smaller than him, as I responded to his comment. "I'm not being a wuss. I just think this is stupid."

He rolled his eyes, a common occurrence with him. "Oh, get over it. All we gotta do is find a stupid piece of junk to prove we came in here. A piece of jewelry, a stuffy old book, anything. Now quit being a baby and come on."

I could only groan as I followed him. That's what I got for hanging out with Benji Banks.

He was a complete moron, yet I tolerated it and had even made him my partner. I had decided a couple of years before that we would be partners, like in detective movies. He was the brawns, and I was the brains. It sounded a lot better than calling another guy—this guy specifically—my friend. The whole school knew it and had no trouble keeping their distance. After all, Benji wasn't exactly someone people liked. But what else was I supposed to do? If I wasn't his "friend," I was a target for his bullying like everyone else, and as I said, he was a fair bit bigger than me and thus also much stronger than me. So long as Benji and I were buddies, no one gave me trouble. Welcome to high school.

That night was another reminder of why I regretted my decision. Benji, being a tough guy, had taken a dare from some other guys at school and ended up dragging me along. The dare was to go inside the abandoned manor in the woods, known as the Cursed Castle of Midnight. It wasn't technically a castle, but it was designed to look like one and the name just kinda worked, I guess.

It was believed that evil spirits lived in the manor after a rich family who once lived there many years ago were murdered. The murderers had never been found, so now everyone believed that if you went inside, you'd be murdered next. I didn't believe in such things, of course. It was just another stupid story kids in my neighborhood had made up to scare one another.

I never really did fit in with the other kids my age. I only moved into town about a year prior, but I never really got comfortable. Maybe it was the fact that my family moved rather often over the course of my life. Making friends was never something I really learned how to do, and no one ever seemed worth the trouble. Any friends I made were more for survival than anything else. Benji was a prime example of that.

I followed Benji into a large dining room. It looked pretty neat for being covered in cobwebs and thick layers of dust and being completely abandoned for who knows how long. The large crystal chandelier above the long, rotted wood table looked incredibly expensive as it hung from the shadowed ceiling. I felt uneasy crossing through that room. The large holes in the ceiling were dark, making me feel as if hidden eyes were watching me from them. It was silly, of course, since I didn't believe in ghosts, but the feeling was strong and made me quick to leave.

Soon we reached a room that was too dark to see in, as there were no windows, so I pulled out my flashlight. Benji was quick to laugh at me for it. "Scaredy-cat! You brought a flashlight? What's wrong, Jason? Scared of the dark?"

I rarely let his words faze me anymore, or anyone's, really. "And exactly how are you going to find something to take back if we can't even see each

THE DARK EXISTENCE

other? Why would I come to an abandoned manor without some kind of light source?"

Benji, of course, rolled his eyes in response.

I looked over the room with my light, revealing where we had found ourselves. Benji grinned as he said, "Looks like we hit the jackpot at least." I guess he was right. We were in an old moth-eaten study. There was a big oak desk to one side and several large shelves of old books around the fairly small room.

I figured just one of those old books would be enough to take back. Sadly, Benji had other ideas. "I bet we could find something really special to take back."

I hated it when he tried to have ideas of his own. "What for? We're just here to grab something to prove we were here and get out! Why in the world would we waste time trying to find something special?"

Benji smirked as he tossed books aside. "Because I wanna see the look on those losers' faces when we bring back the coolest stuff yet! Everyone else who did this dare brought back a lame old book or some stupid spoon! We're gonna make them eat that junk!" He then started searching through the drawers of the old desk.

I simply picked up a book on a nearby end table. "Whatever, man. You do whatever you gotta do. I'll just wait over here. I refuse to dig around in a dead family's belongings just to impress a bunch of dumb jocks with nothing better to do than dare each other to do stupid stuff like this."

THE SILVER SPARROW

I noticed that the title of the book was *Spells and Enchantments*. I opened it and scanned the pages. It was a really old book, but it was in pretty decent shape. It didn't seem to be moth-eaten or molded. In fact, it wasn't in bad shape at all, except that it was fading with age. With a look at the other books, I could see that it seemed in far better shape than any of the other books in that room. Almost like…

"Hey, Benji? Are you sure no one's been here?" I asked as I looked through the pages again.

Benji tossed old papers out of the drawer and moved to another one. "Not since Ted Gabes, and he came two years ago."

We then heard a long creak and stopped what we were doing. We listened for a few seconds before Benji grinned. "Sounds like ghosts."

I felt a little nervous, the unease from the dining room returning for a moment, as I went back to what I was saying. "Then where'd this book come from? It seems too nice to have been here even that long. And we both know Ted hates reading, so why would he leave a book behind?"

Benji ignored me. With a grin, he exclaimed, "Aha! Found something!" He walked over with some shiny object. I pointed my light at what was in his hands and gasped. It was an incredibly beautiful necklace made with gold and rubies. I had never seen anything like it before.

I whistled, just imagining what it was probably worth. "Well, you wanted something special, and you found it."

THE DARK EXISTENCE

He elbowed me and said with a mean grin, "See? Was that so hard? Now we can go. You can go home and cry to your mommy." Yes, that lousy jerk would say that to the guy whose mom has been long dead.

I bit back a remark at that, knowing it wouldn't do me any good. "Let's just go." We both turned to leave.

And we froze.

There stood a girl with long white hair, pale skin like untouched snow, and eyes like radiant jade orbs. If I wasn't so surprised by her sudden appearance, I would have thought she was incredibly beautiful. Her cold grin was not so beautiful. "Don't you know you shouldn't touch a girl's jewelry?"

I'm sure Benji and I would have both screamed if not for someone covering our mouths from behind. The light of my flashlight was enough for us to see a face come up between us. The second figure was a guy around our age, with what I could just barely tell was pale-white skin and dirty blond hair, his bangs hanging over his almost-glowing ruby eyes.

Then a third figure appeared, stepping out of the shadows to stand beside the girl. This guy was huge, with long shaggy hair that was tan in color nearly hiding his rough face and pale-blue eyes. He watched us with a low growl.

The guy holding on to us spoke with a cruel grin. "You naughty little boys are in big trouble now. I thought everyone knew the evil curse on this place, that anyone who goes in is murdered, just as the family who once lived here had been." His grin widened with devious pleasure. "Let me guess. It was a dare, right? That's always it. Everyone we've ever caught said that was it before we"—he came in close to our ears and whispered—"finished them." He licked his teeth. To our utter horror, we saw fangs in his mouth.

I then noticed that the other two weren't as human as we thought either. The other guy had a long tan wolf tail and wolf ears on his head, which I hadn't noticed at first, while the girl carried a long white broomstick at her side. Their grins were all but friendly.

We screamed from behind the vampire's hands and wrenched them off as he laughed. We stood back-to-back, surrounded by the ghouls. I couldn't believe what I was seeing—a vampire, a werewolf, and a witch.

And the worst part was that they had us trapped.

The werewolf stepped closer, making it easier to see him. He even had long nails like claws. As he spoke, he revealed his razor-sharp teeth. "We don't take well to intruders."

I finally found my voice. "Please don't kill us. We swear we didn't mean to intrude. We didn't know. We swear we won't tell anyone anything! You can have the necklace back, and we'll never bother you again or tell anyone what we saw!"

Benji spoke up, sounding even more afraid than me. "What he said!"

The vampire grinned and slouched into a chair. "You wanna know something? I can't stand nosy, whining brats. You sneak around where you have no

THE DARK EXISTENCE

business being, then you wanna cry about it when it blows up in your face. It's honestly really pathetic—too pathetic to deserve to live."

Benji was pale and terrified, a look on him I never could have imagined. "I won't tell anyone! Jason's the pathetic one! You can kill him, and no one would ever know he was gone! Take him!"

Suddenly, he shoved me to the witch's feet and took off screaming. The vampire grinned. With a sigh, he stood up and said, "He ran. He really is pathetic." He gave a chilling grin. "Guess now I'll have to chase him." He then disappeared, moving at a shocking speed.

I stayed on my hands and knees at the witch's feet. I didn't dare look up from the floor.

She finally spoke in a soft, gentle voice. "Why don't you run?"

I spoke almost too quietly to hear without looking up at her. "Would it matter? You'd just chase me too, right?"

The werewolf's voice was gruff, but he really didn't sound much older than me. "Of course."

I felt my blood run cold. "Then just kill me now. Get it over with."

They were silent. I closed my eyes, waiting for the pain and agony to begin. Instead, I got a gruff voice, saying, "Go."

I opened my eyes and looked up at them, surprised. The werewolf spoke again, his voice more like a growl this time. "I said go. Before we change our minds." I stood up hesitantly, not sure what to think. Suddenly, he roared at me, "*Go!*"

I took off out of the room and into the dining room. As I ran for my life, I heard the werewolf yell after me, "Don't ever come back! And if anyone finds out about anything that happened here tonight, we will finish what we started!" I could hear their cruel laughter as I ran out of the dining room.

I stopped when I reached the front hall.

There stood the vampire and Benji in front of the doors. The vampire's head was down on Benji's neck, meaning only one thing. I watched in terror until he raised his head and dropped Benji's body like an empty sack.

He wiped his mouth with his arm when he finally noticed me. He grinned coldly before pushing open the door without taking his eyes off me. The moonlight outside silhouetted him.

I stood there, afraid of going anywhere near him. I glanced at Benji's body on the floor. Seeing that I wasn't moving, the vampire motioned with his arm for me to pass. His grin only grew when I still wouldn't move. I knew that if I was going to die, standing there would do me no good. I finally made my feet move and walked past him, watching him as I went. His eyes followed me out the door.

Once I was out, I ran off. When I was a couple of yards away, I turned back to see the vampire still watching me with that evil grin. I walked further until I was in the shadows of the nearby trees, and once more, I glanced back, hidden from sight.

THE DARK EXISTENCE

That's when I noticed the look of concern and curiosity on his face as if letting me leave made him uneasy. Like it worried him. He glanced back, probably at his partners inside. I didn't understand, but I didn't care to. I quickly ran off for home.

*****

I shuddered at the memory as I sat at my desk. After that night, the police had started a search for Benji, but no one had a clue what happened. When the guys who had dared Benji asked if I had gone with him, I said no. I pretended to not even know anything about the dare.

The guys and I never said a word about it, since that manor was forbidden to all in the first place. They didn't want to become responsible for Benji's disappearance if he had gone to do the dare, but I had far more to fear. Especially when the new kid showed up at school.

He showed up two days after that awful night. That was the day I learned that not all of those monsters had forgotten me.

He had arrived as quietly and mysteriously as a new student could. The teacher hadn't even been able to properly introduce him because he skipped out on it. It was that same afternoon that I learned the truth.

That was Friday. Now it was Monday morning.

I glanced back at the new kid three rows down. I still didn't know his name because I was too busy staying invisible, but I knew who he was already.

THE SILVER SPARROW

He noticed me watching him and grinned. He licked his teeth where his fangs should have been. I immediately turned away.

So, yes. I now had a vampire at my school.

The nightmare had begun, and it would only get worse from there.

JASON

I sat on the bus in my usual spot, the second-to-last row at the back. I had been sitting alone since Benji died. Until that day. That day, someone shoved me into the seat beside me.

My heart caught in my throat as I saw the vampire sitting next to me. I held my backpack to my chest and sat as close to the window as I could. He didn't speak; he only looked me over in silence. He looked me over as if looking for something about me that stood out. I noticed that no one sat very close by, except two guys in the seat in front of us.

The vampire turned his attention to them as he stood up and looked down at them. "Get lost."

The guys glared back. "Or what?"

He gave them an evil glare, which shut them up fast. They even went two rows up, leaving me alone in the back of the bus with the vampire. He glanced at me again as he sat down as if expecting me to say something about it, but I turned and looked out the window. Maybe if I was quiet and invisible, he wouldn't bother with me.

As the bus drove off, I could feel his eyes on me again. "What's your name?"

I was hesitant, but I gave my answer. "Jason Conner."

The vampire was quiet, but only for a moment. "How old are you?"

I answered again, "I'm seventeen."

He was silent again. Then he asked, "Any family?"

"A little brother and my dad."

"Any talents?"

"Not really."

He groaned and got up close to me, making me shrink back from him. He looked me in the eyes, and I looked into his. If I looked hard enough, I could see that his eyes were red instead of auburn.

Finally, he hissed softly in irritation, "I don't get it."

I didn't understand. "What are you talking about?"

He kept his eyes on me. "Why didn't they kill you? Why you?"

I suddenly realized who he was talking about—the witch and the werewolf. He was wondering why they didn't kill me.

The vampire looked really ticked. "I just don't get it! We never let you idiots live before! Why now? Why you?"

I couldn't answer him. Honestly, I was wondering that too. Why didn't they just kill me?

He backed off and slumped in the seat again. I watched him, wondering why he didn't know. Why didn't he just ask them? Why come to my school and ask me?

I sighed and looked out the window again. I guess I felt a little relieved to know he hadn't come to the school to kill me; he just came to get answers.

After about twenty minutes, we reached my stop. I turned to the vampire, who had fallen asleep with his knees against the seat in front of us. I hesitantly tapped his shoulder. "Uh, hey."

He opened his eyes and noticed we had stopped.

I felt the chill again, but I managed to speak. "Uh, this is my stop."

The vampire, to my relief, sat up so his legs were out of the way for me to pass.

I walked to the door of the bus but stopped and looked back. "Uh, by the way."

The vampire glanced at me, slumped in the seat again.

I cleared my throat. "I was just wondering what your name was."

He looked me over, expressionless, then spoke. "Vince."

I found that a little more relieving, knowing he had an average name. It made him seem a little less evil.

I stepped off the bus and watched it drive off. Vince the vampire. I had a feeling that wasn't the last I would see of him.

VINCE

I groaned. I was sitting in my room in the manor. It was a very fancy bedroom but in total shambles, just the way I liked it. The others had the nicer rooms. No surprise. Sethra was always so high-maintenance, and that Jamal was such a royal wuss.

Just thinking about him irritated me. I really couldn't stand him, but I had to get over it. He was part of the plan, and I wanted this plan to work. Though I was starting to have my doubts. Something else was going down, and I wanted to find out what. Sethra and Jamal were hiding something from me.

Figures. Those two were two peas in a pod. At least, that's what puppy-boy thought. As far as he knew, he and Sethra were in it together to the end. They were, as they put it, *partners*.

Poor, pathetic lovesick puppy. He was far too attached to that witch. Being a vampire, I didn't really trust anybody, especially not witches like little Miss Sethra.

I tossed a tennis ball at the wall, letting it bounce back into my hand as I leaned back in my chair. I had kept the tennis ball from that old school. That made me think of the mortal kid.

THE DARK EXISTENCE

Jason Conner.

Seventeen and in a family of three. That was it? He had no special importance, even by mortal standards. So why didn't Sethra and Jamal kill him? I knew this had to do with that secret they were keeping from me.

As a vampire, I usually found mysteries exciting, but this was a mystery that bothered me deeply. What could they possibly be hiding from me? And why? I doubt they even knew I was on to them. They didn't give me any credit since I was just a vampire. Werewolves and witches don't mix well with vampires. Honestly, no night creature really does.

I caught the ball one last time and glanced outside. From the strength of my senses, I surmised that it was probably about three in the morning. Being a vampire gave me a connection to the night, making me stronger. I could tell what time it was just by the height of my strength. The closer to midnight, the higher my strength, but as it got closer to dawn, my strength would go down as well.

I sighed. I had to get answers out of those two.

And I knew just how to do it.

JASON

I felt a thud in my chest as Vince sat at the lunch table with me. The few other kids who were sitting with me quickly moved out when he walked over. Now we were alone. He looked me over, again wondering if I'd do something about it. Of course, I didn't. He pulled out a spork and opened a little plastic container of soaking sliced peaches. "It's Jason Conner, right?"

I managed to get a word out as I stirred my pudding with my spork, not looking at him. "Yeah."

He ate a peach slice as he leaned back. "When you entered the manor, it was for a dare, right?"

I nodded.

He thought as he ate another slice. Then he asked, "Who was that kid with you?"

I felt a chill down my spine. I had refused to think about Benji since that night. I didn't really care about him or even like him, but I still felt pretty bad he had to die like that. No one even knew.

I finally found my voice. "Benji Banks. He's the one who talked me into doing that dare with him."

Vince opened his milk carton. "Anything special about him?"

THE DARK EXISTENCE

He got killed by a vampire, I thought, but I figured that didn't count. I shook my head. "Just another dork who thought he could rule the world. People like him always have that flaw. They always forget they're only human."

Vince seemed to think on that as if my words meant something to him. Finally, he sighed as he ate. "You really do confuse me, kid."

I was surprised. "I do?"

He closed his eyes and leaned back in his chair. "Well, not necessarily you. More the fact that you're still here."

I realized he was still on that question. Why wasn't I killed that night? I found myself talking without quite as much hesitation. "How come you don't just ask the witch girl or the werewolf guy?"

He groaned as if it were a sore topic to him. "Because I know they're purposely keeping it from me. They're hiding something, and you're part of it. I just don't know what."

I found that even more surprising. "Why would they keep secrets from you?"

Vince looked concerned. "Beats me. Their kinds never got along with mine, so it's probably the issue of trust."

I was quiet as I thought about it. It sounded a lot like the mystery novels I read.

But wait. This wasn't some mystery novel. This was my life, now including ghouls who wanted to kill me! The last thing I wanted was to bother asking questions about why I wasn't killed. I was lucky and

THE SILVER SPARROW

perfectly happy with not knowing. I was getting in too deep. It wasn't worth it!

I shook my head and ate some pudding.

Vince seemed to notice. "Scared?"

I immediately wondered if he, like in some stories about vampires, could read my mind.

He smirked as he watched my face. "Yeah, it's obvious you are."

I looked at my pudding. "Well, when you know three ghouls exist and one of them is hanging over your shoulder, you find yourself a little on edge."

Vince burst out laughing, something I had never seen him do. I had seen him in his mischievous delight, but never simple, ordinary amusement. He sighed and said with a grin, "You are definitely mortal. You have no clue."

He stood up and dumped his lunch, which he had barely touched, in the garbage. He turned to me and leaned in, just enough for me to hear him whisper, "Meet me on Creven Hill tonight at midnight. Don't be late and don't even think of telling anyone, or I'll find you and kill you next." He gave me that evil grin and walked off.

It was after he was out of sight that I realized I was holding my breath. I released it and looked down at my hands. As normal as he tended to seem, I couldn't let myself forget he was a murderous vampire.

And I was on his list.

VINCE

I sat in the tree, waiting. It was about midnight, and that kid hadn't shown up yet. I wasn't worried though. I knew he'd show up sooner or later. He wasn't the type to get on anyone's bad side. He was a smart kid, not at all like his little buddy Benji. I grinned at the memory of chasing that big oaf and his screams.

Now the question was, where were my little partners? I sighed and leaned back. I sat along a large branch up high.

Then my strong hearing caught the sound of footfalls coming in my direction. I looked in the direction of the steps, knowing who it was by how little they tried to hide the sound.

That was when Jason stepped out of the shadows of the trees. He looked around quietly. I could tell he was nervous and probably terrified, yet he kept an impressively cool head. He stood there, looking around for me.

I remembered when he had entered the manor. I had watched him and his little friend walk in, from where I had hidden in the rafters of the dining room. It was the perfect hiding place, which I had learned in the past. No one ever checks above.

THE SILVER SPARROW

I slipped off the branch soundlessly and landed on the ground behind him, nearly dead silent. Jason still felt my presence and jumped with a little spin. I smirked. "For someone who looks so coolheaded, you sure are jumpy."

He sighed, calming down. "Well, your kind has that effect on people."

I chuckled darkly. That was very true.

Then two others stepped out of the shadows. I had expected them to show up first, but obviously, they took their time, since they never took me seriously.

I also noticed that Jamal was in his husky werewolf form again. No doubt being prepared in case I tried anything with him or his little girlfriend. As I said, these two never trusted me.

Sethra sighed in that way that only proved she was high-maintenance. "What are we doing here, Vince? And please make it quick."

I glanced at her. "I want answers."

She raised a thin eyebrow at me. "Answers?"

I stuffed my hands into my pockets as I faced her. "Yeah, answers. Several, actually."

She sighed as she brushed her bangs from her eyes. "I don't know what you're talking about, vampire."

I pointed an accusing finger at her. "Knock it off, witch! I'm not stupid. I know you're keeping secrets from me. Just what are you hiding? What's really your plan, Sethra?"

Jamal growled at me, "Watch your tongue, vampire. She's kept no secrets. She's told you her plans—*our* plans."

I waved him off, annoyed by his obliviousness. "Oh shut up, you idiot. You wouldn't know a liar if they made out with you, which she has."

He growled angrily at me.

I knew he was madly in love with Sethra, but I also knew it was that very love that kept him in the dark of her true intentions. I wasn't blind like him. I could see she was hiding something, and I was going to find out what.

She didn't give anything away. "As Jamal said, I've told you everything. I know you were the latest part of all this, but I'd have thought you'd have understood it by now."

I hated how she made me look so stupid. "Forget it, witch. I already told you, I'm not fooled. You may not think my kind is capable of being very bright, but we are by far the best at sniffing out a rotten witch."

Jamal took a step toward me, but Sethra held her hand out for him to stop. He stayed where he was. Sethra was always the one in charge, but I found that made her only that much more dangerous.

She looked at me with those powerful green eyes. "Now, Vince, why don't you explain what has you so on edge this lovely night?" Now she was patronizing? Oh, how I hated that witch.

I glared at her. "Fine, how about answering this question for me?" I grabbed Jason's arm and held him

THE SILVER SPARROW

where they could see him. "Why didn't you kill this kid? I know you have a reason."

Sethra looked intrigued. "That's what you've been doing this last week? Searching for him? I was starting to wonder."

She was getting off the subject, but I wasn't going to have that. "Why'd you both let him go? Why didn't you kill him?"

Sethra shrugged casually. "We didn't care."

I scoffed. "Oh, please. We've killed every nitwit that's ever entered the manor for the last year we've been there, but with this one, you just didn't care to kill him?"

She crossed her arms, looking tired of this conversation. "What does it matter, Vince? If you want to kill him, then kill him."

I looked her over, curious and cautious.

She smirked at my hesitation. "What? Now you *don't* want to kill him?"

Jamal laughed.

Sethra watched me with that dark smile I never trusted. "Well? Go ahead. Kill him."

I watched them, then glanced at Jason.

He saw my look and paled. "Oh, please don't."

Before he could say another word, his shoulders were in my grip and my fangs in his neck. It only took a few seconds, then I dropped him with a soft thud. I kicked him into the shadows and wiped my mouth with my wrist. I turned back to the other two.

Sethra grinned darkly. "Feel better?"

THE DARK EXISTENCE

I didn't answer; I only watched them. Something was still wrong. The way she smiled, the way Jamal watched me—there was something else.

Then Sethra spoke up out of nowhere. "You know, you ask a lot of questions, vampire. You doubt my ways and even seem to defy them."

Suddenly, I found myself struggling to breathe.

She gave me an evil grin. "I hate it."

My muscles grew incredibly weak, and I fell to my knees. I tried to hold myself up, trying desperately to breathe, but I was failing. It felt like my throat was closing up entirely. I felt my body sweating as it seemed to heat up from the inside. I finally collapsed to my side, barely managing faint breaths.

Sethra came and stood over me, watching my suffering with devious pleasure. She knelt down and caressed my face with her gentle hands. "I'm afraid you will no longer be of much use to our cause. You're too defiant and… willful."

I knew what she meant clearly. She didn't like that I was thinking and acting for myself. I knew she wouldn't.

She gave me a beautiful smile. "Too bad. This is what happens when you don't trust, vampire. Instead of continuing forward with us, you'll just have to lie here alone to die." She stood up with a dark yet alluring smile. "As for what I've been keeping to myself, it's really quite simple. I knew you wouldn't approve. Jamal didn't at first, but he trusts me with all his heart now. You see, for our plan to work, sacrifices will have to be made."

I wondered as my breathing was completely cut off. *What sacrifices? What evil plan could this witch have cooked up that even Jamal didn't approve of in his right mind?*

She grinned as she watched the stars above. "I wonder just how big an army you could have with more night creatures and less mortals?" She laughed and walked away. Jamal looked at me once more, then followed her. I was left there, falling unconscious. As everything faded out, one last thought crossed my mind.

That lousy witch.

JASON

I lay there in the shadows, waiting for my body to wake up. I had heard every word but didn't quite understand. What plan? What army? And what did she mean by "more night creatures and less mortals"? I could only lie there thinking about it in my numb body.

I still didn't understand why I wasn't dead—again. I felt Vince drink my blood. As he drank, my body had grown weak and numb, rising from my hands and feet, up my body, and toward my head, as if my spirit had been rising out through the top of my body.

However, just as the numbness had reached my neck, he had dropped me and kicked me aside. I guess I could now say I knew what it felt like to be only a head. I mean, I couldn't feel a thing in my body. However, as the hours went by, my body slowly came back. The dark sky was growing lighter by the time I could get up. My toes and the tips of my fingers were still numb, but at least I could move.

My entire body ached as I stood up, careful not to lose my balance. As I stretched, I saw Vince not too far off. I walked over and looked down at his dead body.

However, something in my gut told me he probably wasn't dead. He was a vampire after all. I didn't believe it was that easy to kill one, at least not without a stake or a beheading.

I saw how bright the sky was getting and immediately thought of something. If he was a vampire, didn't that mean the sunlight would kill him? Sethra did say he was supposed to lie there to die. If whatever she did to him didn't kill him, maybe she had meant for the sunlight to. After all, he only ever looked like his vampire self when it was dark out. Otherwise, he looked human, and he definitely didn't look like that now.

I hesitantly lifted Vince up, throwing his arm over my neck, and headed for home with him. As insane as I felt, something told me it was okay to help him. For some reason, I wasn't afraid of him anymore—at least, not as scared as I should have been. It was like a wave of courage washed over me.

I had just reached the front path of my house when the sun peeked out from beyond the horizon. I gasped as I reached the door. Vince's skin was starting to burn in the sunlight. His blond hair started to fade, and he looked to be in massive pain—so much pain that I could feel his body tense up, proving me right about him being alive after all.

I hurried him into the house and laid him on the floor. I quickly closed the door and all the curtains, leaving us in a decently dark front hall. Vince didn't seem to be burning anymore, but the damage already done was still there. Spots of his pale skin were bright red or already turning a dark ugly color, his hair was a dull shade, and I noticed that the areas around his eyes were slightly purple. I knew I had to do something, but what?

Then I remembered something I had read in a story once. I hurried into the kitchen and picked up a small but sharp knife. I held it and felt insane. What was I doing? What was I thinking? I had to have lost my mind, I thought as I stood over Vince. But as I looked at him, for some reason, I just couldn't stand to watch him die.

I groaned and cut my hand, careful not to cut anything too severe. I held back my reaction to the pain and let my blood drip into Vince's mouth. After a moment, he started to move. Then he started gasping for air as if his throat was opening up. His burns started to fade away, and his hair returned to its original color. Clearly, it did the trick.

He stayed unconscious as I wrapped my hand. Then I carried him upstairs to my room as quietly as possible. I didn't want to wake my little brother. Who knew how he'd react? I had to keep this quiet until I could fix it. No big deal, right?

Dead wrong.

JASON

I was sitting at my desk chair when I heard Vince groan. I stood up and walked over to the side of my bed, where he was lying. He groaned again as he slowly came back to consciousness. My curtains, which were pretty thick, were closed. I thought I saw him open his eyes and look around. He sounded puzzled when he finally spoke. "Where am I?"

I answered softly, so as not to spook him or something. "At my house."

He looked surprised. "Jason?"

I smiled. "Yeah. You okay?"

He still looked puzzled, though now there was a hint of worry. "What's going on?"

I tried to be comforting; after all, he did just get betrayed by his partners. "You were almost killed by that witch and werewolf."

He waved it off. "No, I remember that. I mean why can't I see?"

I spoke as I looked over at the thick curtains. "Oh, I closed the curtains to keep the sunlight out. They make it pretty dark—"

THE DARK EXISTENCE

He cut me off as he sat up, sounding very worried and impatient. "No, I can see perfectly in the dark. Why can't I see now?"

I was surprised.

Sounding really worried now, he asked, "What happened?"

I recounted everything after what happened on the hill, which didn't take all that long, until I reached the end. "Then I brought you to my house for safety. We made it just as the sun was coming up."

He pondered on it, though I noticed he was looking straight ahead. Suddenly, he looked horrified. "Oh no." He covered his face and shook his head. "Oh no, no, no."

I was curious as to what was wrong. "What is it?"

He uncovered his face. "I must have looked at the sun."

I didn't get it. "But you recovered after I gave you blood."

He shook his head again. "No, I mean I looked *directly* at the *sun*. Because of it, I'm now blind."

So much for saving him.

Then he looked surprised. "Wait. You gave me blood?" He turned in my direction but didn't look at me directly. "From where?"

I felt stupid as I remembered. "From my hand. I sorta cut it and gave you some blood so you wouldn't die."

Vince looked surprised. "You did that? What for? I almost killed you."

Then it suddenly hit me why I had saved him. "Because you didn't kill me. I know it was on purpose. You let me live, even when you could have just killed me. On the hill, you only drank enough blood to make it look like I was dead. I easily recovered after that."

He looked pretty thoughtful for the scary vampire I'd been seeing over the last week.

After a moment, he smirked. "Yeah, well, that was only because Sethra wanted me to kill you. I knew she was up to something. She wanted me to kill you a little too much for not having done it herself. By drinking your blood, I also got her magic over you too. She probably put it on you before she let you leave that first night. That's why she let you live. You were a foolproof way to get rid of me."

I was surprised. "Wait, she put magic on me that night? That's why they let me live?"

Vince nodded. "Witch magic is deadly to vampires, even harmless magic."

I found that very interesting.

He smirked. "Too bad for them, it didn't work." Then he looked a little bummed. "Not quite, anyway."

I couldn't help feeling bad. "Sorry about that."

He sighed and said with a shrug, "Doesn't matter. It's just blindness. I can still hear extremely well, and my other senses are still perfectly fine. No real harm done."

I had to smile. He was a pretty optimistic guy, for a vampire.

THE DARK EXISTENCE

He climbed off the bed and stretched. "So this is your place, huh?"

I nodded. Then I wanted to hit myself, and I spoke. "Yeah, we're in my room right now."

He smirked as he seemed to look around, though I figured he was listening. "You mean to tell me you carried me all the way to your house? In the dark? Alone?"

I smiled, a little embarrassed. "Well, yeah. It would have been kinda hard getting help for a vampire." He laughed, but I suddenly shushed him. "Be quiet, or my little brother will hear you."

He quieted down. "Oh, right. You have a family. Daddy-o a deep sleeper?"

I scoffed. "We don't have to worry about him, because he's not even here. He never is. It's just my little brother and me right now. Dad works almost 24-7. Even now, he's traveling for work."

Vince thought about it, his sightless eyes staring straight ahead. "Oh. You have one of *those* dads. Lame."

I had to agree. It was pretty lame.

He sighed as he rubbed his chin. "Now about those two." He crossed his arms, looking pretty ticked off as he thought to himself. "I'm gonna kill them. I'm gonna rip them to pieces and then feed those pieces to hellhounds."

I gulped. "Hellhounds?"

He nodded, not at all fazed by the words coming out of his mouth. "Yeah, I know a guy who's got three."

I groaned. "What other nonexistent things actually exist?"

I didn't really mean it as a question, but Vince snickered. "If I told you that, you may never feel safe in the dark again."

I knew he was right.

Then he sighed, sounding more serious. "Though I can't do anything to those two traitors just yet. There's something I still need to figure out first."

I felt the same way. "Yeah, what did she mean by 'more night creatures and less mortals'?"

Vince felt for a chair and sat in it. "Well, obviously, it means she's gonna get rid of mortals so she can have more night creatures. I bet she plans to use Hallows' Eve to do it."

I was surprised. "Hallows' Eve? You mean Halloween? That's next week."

He nodded and leaned back. "Before I explain that to you, first you have to understand where we come from." He closed his eyes and thought about it a moment before he finally spoke. "We, simply called night creatures, exist in a realm called the Hallows Realm. It hides in the mortal world where you can't see it. It's like… well, it's like a pocket in your reality."

That sounded kinda awesome. "Cool."

Vince continued, "On Hallows' Eve, that pocket, which is our realm, opens a little connection into your world. This opening, something like a tear in the fabric of reality, is small, and only a few night creatures come out to haunt the mortals. But by midnight, we all return, and the connection is closed. For the last seven years, there has been unbalance in our realm, causing *things* to happen. One of those *things* is holes in our pockets that let night creatures into your world all year round. That's how Sethra, Jamal, and I got here. The original connection may not be open, but now it's not necessary if we want to enter your world."

I shivered as I sat on the edge of my bed. "That sounds awful. What caused the imbalance?"

Vince groaned. "That would be the fault of the King of Night. He rules the Night Kingdom of the Hallows Realm. The Night Kingdom is the largest land of our world, and it sits at the very center. Every hundred years, the present King of Night hands the crown to the next chosen. Each ruler keeps the crown for one hundred years exactly and then passes it on. But this time, the King of Night refused to give up his crown. He believed he was the only one suitable to rule, and because he was so incredibly powerful, no one could stop him. And so the unbalance began, from night creatures becoming more aggressive, to the holes that let night creatures loose on the mortal world, to even alterations to the realm itself!"

I lay back across the bed. "Sounds like one selfish king. And there's no one who can stop him?"

Vince shrugged. "There are some, but they'd be taking one heck of a risk trying. They're smart, so they just try to keep the King of Night in line as best they can while seeking out a way to make him give up his crown. That's what Jamal, Sethra, and I were doing."

I looked at him. "So that's what you're all trying to do? Make him give up his crown?"

Vince nodded.

I found myself curious about this plan of theirs. "And just what was that plan?"

He was quiet for a moment, then he answered, "We were trying to gather as many witches, wizards, werewolves, and vampires as we could to stand up against the King of Night. We knew that if we could show him how many of us he'd have to face to keep his crown, he'd give up. Sethra, being a very powerful witch, could gather other witches and wizards easily. Jamal, being a werewolf tribe leader, could gather loyal werewolves. And I, being a highly respected vampire around the realm and also very talented in persuasion, could persuade other vampires. After all, magic wielders, werewolves, and vampires are the original races of the Hallows Realm, making us the majority races and some of the most powerful. It's why our kinds are called the origin races. Sethra said it was foolproof, but apparently, that wasn't her full plan. She's up to far more than that."

I watched him, feeling uneasy all of a sudden. "And just what was the rest of her plan?"

Vince looked grim. "She's trying to build an army. She's going to start a war, and she's going to do it in the most heinous way possible." He turned in my direction. "On Hallows' Eve, when the connection opens, she's going to start turning mortals into night creatures to join her army."

THE DARK EXISTENCE

I felt my heart stop. "What? Is that even possible?"

He crossed his arms. "There's a spell to do it. That's what she meant by 'more night creatures and less mortals.' It would make her army unstoppable. Of course, it's extremely forbidden, and I'm a little shocked myself that she would even dare use a magic that dangerous. But she is kinda stupid, so it shouldn't be that surprising. Unfortunate, but not surprising."

I couldn't even grasp that thought. "That's horrible! We can't let that happen!"

Vince raised an eyebrow. "We?"

I stood up as a wave of courage washed over me. "We're going to stop her!"

He looked surprised. "Dang. When'd you get all brave?"

I grinned. "I have no clue, but I'm gonna put it to use! We're gonna kick that sorry witch's butt!"

Vince jumped to his feet, surprisingly excited. "Heck yeah! I'm game!" He grinned. "You know, when you're not a total mortal loser, you're a pretty cool kid. I could get used to having you as a witch-butt-kicking partner."

I felt a little surprised, then I grinned. "Then I guess we're partners." He shook my hand, but then I pulled him close. "But if you try to kill me, I'll make you lose more than just your sight. I know your weakness now, and I will use it."

He looked surprised at first, but then he gave a cool grin. "Can't argue with that. You did save my life after all. I guess you've got my respect. And when it comes to vampires, respect is everything." I let go of his hand, and he chuckled. "Maybe you'll do well in the Hallows Realm."

I looked at him. "What do you mean? Aren't they at the manor?"

Vince laughed. "Are you nuts? We can't just go barging into the castle to fight off a witch and a werewolf! Sethra is one of the most cunning witches in the Hallows Realm, and don't even get me started on wolf-boy. No, we'd be dead before we reached the front door."

I stuffed my hands into my pockets. "So then, what are we going to do?"

He grinned. "We're gonna go get a little help from some old friends. I know some people who would happily help us kick little Miss Sethra's butt."

I raised an eyebrow. "Who?"

His grin widened. "Her sisters."

JASON

I suddenly found myself underwater. Or I thought it was water. I finally managed to pull myself up to breathe, to find that it was above my waist and that it was *not* water. I looked around and saw that I was in a swamp. And that "water" was so muddy that I refused to call it water of any kind.

Then I saw a hand reach out beside me, and I pulled him up. Vince gasped for air as I helped him to his feet. "Okay, maybe I was wrong. There are some downsides to being blind. I can't see where the heck is up when I'm underwater!" I couldn't help but smile. Then I looked up at the dark twilight sky above us.

Believe it or not, we were in the Hallows Realm.

Vince had taken me to one of the "holes" that connected our two worlds, and that was how we ended up there. We hadn't been expecting such an unfortunate spot to appear in though.

He wiped the swamp mud/water off his face. "All right, so obviously we're in the Southern Swamps. Can you see a house anywhere?" His eyes were dull gold now, which I only noticed once we were in some light.

THE SILVER SPARROW

Right now, he was back in his vampire form. When we had left the house, he had looked like he did in school. That, as he told me, was the only way he could withstand the sunlight, much like what I figured out. Using a special token he had, some small piece of metal that supposedly had magic, he could change into a mortal form. But since it was dark out now, he was his vampire self again.

I looked around. It looked exactly as I always imagined a swamp would look. Though I didn't see any houses, only trees and more muddy ponds nearby. That's when I noticed a faint glow of light. "No, but I think I see lights to the left of here."

Vince sighed. "All right, then that's where we have to go." He started wading through the muck, and I followed.

I started thinking about David, my little brother. I had him stay with an aunt who lived nearby, but I didn't tell him why or where I was going. As far as he probably knew, I was going to hang out with Benji or some guys I knew.

Finally, we got on some solid, dry ground. I managed to get most of that muck off before we headed toward the lights. Vince spoke as he followed me by the sound of my steps. "Keep your eyes open for a house that sorta looks like a pumpkin with a witch's hat on." I found that to be an interesting description, but once I saw the house, nothing could have described it better.

There sat a cute cottage that was shaped and painted like a pumpkin, and the roof looked like a witch's pointed hat that bent over halfway up and curled inward at the very tip. The windows were even shaped like the eyes of a jack-o'-lantern. Little orange lawn lights were set up around the house, making the cottage look like it was glowing. I finally said, "Dude, I think I found it."

He grinned. "Kid, if you found it, you won't have to *think* anything."

Well, that was that. "Then it's definitely the one."

He laughed and walked up to the door, which wasn't hard since there were voices coming from inside. He stood before the door, put on a handsome grin, and then knocked. The door was soon opened by an incredibly beautiful woman. Her long hair was dark blue, and her eyes matched beautifully.

Vince grinned alluringly. "Surprise!"

She smiled with excitement, making her midnight-blue eyes sparkle. "Vince!" She turned toward the inside of the house. "Girls! Guess who's here?"

She grabbed Vince's hand and pulled him inside. I followed him in and was immediately hit by a million and one smells. They were all amazing. There were herbs, cakes, fruit, and any other wonderful smell you could think of in a cottage shaped like a pumpkin. The house was really one big room. There were four beds along one wall, a kitchen set up on the other side, a cabinet full of odds and ends, and a large cauldron in the center of the room. There was a table on one side of the room covered in sweets, cakes, and other treats, and herbs hung from the ceiling.

THE SILVER SPARROW

The woman pulled Vince over toward the cauldron, where two other women were. One had long gorgeous blond hair and scarlet eyes, while the other witch looked older than the first two, with violet hair and matching eyes that were old and wise. Unlike the other ladies, she didn't wear a witch's hat, but I noticed a red witch hat on one of the beds.

She was stirring the cauldron as the second witch smiled excitedly. "Vince!" She ran over and took his other hand. I grinned. Guess it wasn't only at school that all the girls fell all over him.

Vince grinned. "Ladies, it's great to see—uh, *be* here with you again." I noticed he had been about to say "see you," which bummed me out a little.

That was when the first witch gasped. "Why, Vince, whatever happened to your eyes?"

He sighed as he let her turn his face to hers. "You can thank your sweet little sister for that."

They suddenly started glowing. Seriously! Each of them had a red glow to them like they were seething at the memory of their sister!

The first witch managed to speak, still holding Vince's hand. "Sethra. That little twit girl."

The second witch still had his other hand. "How dare she bring harm to our darling vampire prince!"

Vince gave that charming grin of his. "It's all right, ladies. Don't you worry. I'm just fine. Your vampire prince is still alive and well. Well, half alive anyway."

I grinned, getting the vampire joke.

THE DARK EXISTENCE

Suddenly, I felt a little zap in my stomach, and everything changed. I blinked to find that everything around me was huge. Then I looked at myself. No. It was me who shrank. I was a mouse! I gasped, but out came a squeak.

Vince must have heard it. "What was that?"

The eldest witch walked over, lifting the hem of her dress as she came. The click of her heels was much louder to my little mouse ears. She reached down for me, but I took off with another round of *squeak, squeak*.

Vince groaned as he listened. "Jason, please tell me you're not a mouse." I squeaked again as I ran from the witch, who was still trying to grab me. Hearing my squeaks, he turned toward me as I ran to him. He quickly picked me up before the witch could grab my tail. I hid in his cupped hands, afraid of what a witch planned to do with a mouse. Probably cook me in some stew, I assumed.

The older witch grinned at Vince. "Friend of yours?"

Vince smiled at her, though his eyes looked past her. "Yes, he is. Afraid you can't have him. I still need him."

She sighed and said with a clever old-woman smile, "All right. I guess I'll have to go find my own for my stew tonight." I called it!

She pulled out a wand as she stepped back. "You might want to put him down, dear."

Vince set me on the floor, and the witch waved her wand. Suddenly, I was tall again and standing beside Vince. I noticed that he and I were suddenly clean too.

He gave a polite bow. "Thank you, my dear Melora."

The witch, Melora, smiled. "Only for you, Vince." She walked back over to her cauldron. "So what has our little sister done this time?"

Vince sighed. "Seems she's trying to lead a war against the King of Night."

The witches all gasped and looked at him in surprise.

The blue-haired witch pulled up a chair. "Here you go, Vince."

Vince sat down with a grateful smile. "Thanks, Berleen."

She giggled pleasantly.

The blond witch kindly pulled out a chair for me too. "And for the friend of Vince."

I smiled and sat in the chair. "Thank you."

She smiled back, with a soft blush to her cheeks. "You can call me Leanndra."

I gave my most charming smile. "Thank you, Leanndra. That's a very beautiful name."

She blushed and said with a giggle, "Oh, stop!"

She and Berleen had to be in their late twenties, but they still acted like young schoolgirls. Vince nudged me with his elbow as he grinned.

Melora sighed as she leaned on the long wooden spoon she was stirring with. "That Sethra. She always was power-hungry, but I had hoped it would pass with time and age."

Berleen and Leanndra nodded sullenly.

Melora looked at us. "And just what did this have to do with you, Vince? And I'm sure your mortal friend here has ties to this as well?"

Berleen and Leanndra gasped. "Mortal?"

Berleen then smiled. "I thought he was a vampire, but I guess he really doesn't look like one."

Leanndra giggled. "I honestly thought he was a werewolf."

Berleen put her fists to her hips. "And why would you think he's a werewolf? You know Vince can't stand werewolves!"

Leanndra just shrugged and said with a smile, "Well, he's just as handsome as one. And sweet!"

Vince laughed. "I guess you should take that as a compliment, kid."

I blinked at him. "But I thought you didn't like werewolves."

He grinned. "I don't, but girls sure as heck do. Werewolves are extremely handsome in mortal form, and almost no girl can resist them! For Leanndra to think you're a werewolf, you must be a serious looker in their eyes." He then shrugged. "Don't see why. You didn't seem that special when I could see you."

I grinned at the witches. "Well, thank you, ladies."

Leanndra and Berleen got all giddy, like girls meeting members of their favorite boy band. Though I found it odd that werewolves were believed to be very handsome. Jamal sure wasn't.

Melora sighed, bored with her sisters. "Will you two grow up? Sethra got over that phase years ago. Even Melody is past that."

The two sisters pouted.

Vince grinned. "Say, where is your little angel?"

Just then, a young voice spoke from the door. "I'm home."

I looked to see a girl maybe one or two years younger than me. She had long purple hair with a big blue bow and big purple eyes. She was calm and quiet but looked just like Melora.

Melora smiled. "There you are, dear. Did you find what I asked for?"

The girl walked over to her. "Yes, mother."

Melora accepted the little basket. "Wonderful. Did you find it all right?"

The girl nodded politely. "Yes, it wasn't hard to find."

Melora kissed her head, clearly very proud of her. "Thank you very much, Melody."

Melody then noticed Vince. "Hello, Vince."

Vince grinned. "Hey, Melody. Still as pretty as your mom?"

She gave a small smile. "Yes, so I'm told." She could see he was blind now.

Vince decided to get back on topic. "Well, as for Sethra's plans, she's actually planning to use *the spell* on Hallows' Eve."

The sisters gasped. "What?"

He nodded. "And if she manages to do it, then war will break out."

THE DARK EXISTENCE

Melora looked grim. "So she's finally learned that awful spell. Must have found the book after all."

Leanndra looked worried but not surprised. "You always did say she would."

Melora nodded. "I had hoped I would be wrong. With that book, more than just that terrible spell will be at her disposal. I can't imagine what all she's already learned from it by now. Where did she even manage to find one, I wonder?"

As they spoke, I noticed Melody was watching me. I gave her a smile and a little wave, trying to be friendly. She blushed and looked away, though I noticed a tiny smile. It seemed her aunts weren't the only ones who had a thing for me.

Vince sighed, bringing me back into the conversation. "As much as I love your company, ladies, I was hoping you could help me out. See, I have a little payback to take care of, which includes crushing Sethra's chances of success. You ladies wouldn't mind helping a guy out, would you? For little old me?"

They glanced at each other, then grinned at him.

Melora did the talking. "There is one way you could stop her in time. The one thing that stopped the use of that book in the past."

Vince waited for the answer. "What would that be?"

She smiled. "The Sorcerer's Crown."

He was surprised. "The Sorcerer's Crown? But I thought that was impossible!"

THE SILVER SPARROW

Melora's smile was a bit devious. "Not anymore." She glanced at me.

I wondered what she meant, but Berleen spoke up. "Though we don't know much about it, there is one witch who could help you!"

Melora smiled. "Do you still see Rose, Vince?"

He grinned, strangely a bit excited. "Sure, I still see Rose!" Then his smile wavered. "Well, I *could* see her."

Melora continued. "She may know more that could help you."

Vince sighed and stood up. "All right, then I guess we're heading to StarLight Hills."

I got to my feet too. "StarLight Hills?"

He nodded and headed for the door. "That's where Rose now lives with the—"

Suddenly, he walked into the doorframe. The ladies and I couldn't help but laugh. He rubbed his nose. "Dang it. Not funny."

I pushed him along through the door. "Thanks a lot, ladies."

They said bye together as I closed the door behind us.

Vince groaned. "I'm really starting to hate being blind."

I smirked as I led him away, having him avoid the lawn ornaments. "Well, then I guess you're glad to have me around as your eyes."

He shrugged. "I guess. At least I have that. Better than wandering around with no clue where the heck I'm going."

THE DARK EXISTENCE

I glanced back at the cute pumpkin cottage and saw Melody watching us through the window. I gave her a wave as I smiled at her. She blushed and waved back with a sweet smile. I knew I had to be blushing a little too. She was kinda cute.

Vince stopped and put a hand to my face. I pulled it away, not appreciating it in the least. "Okay, hands off, man."

He grinned. "I can't see, but I can feel. You've got the hots for Melody!"

I blushed more. "No way. Now can we focus? Where's StarLight Hills?"

Vince grinned but moved on. "Walk straight ahead from the left of the house."

I led him to the left side of the cottage and started walking forward. I let him go once he got a handle on which direction we were going.

He stuffed his hands into his pockets as we walked toward the edge of the swamp. "Well, I guess I ought to explain some things to you now."

I could certainly agree with that. "Yeah, like what was all that about? How are you so close to Sethra's sisters? And are you really a vampire prince?"

Vince laughed. "Those are your questions? That's it? Okay, well, I know her sisters because they've always had a soft spot for me. We met years ago, and they found me exciting and handsome. Meeting them is how I came to meet Sethra in the first place. And, no, I'm not a prince. They just call me their vampire prince, like a 'You're my knight in shining armor' thing."

THE SILVER SPARROW

I grinned. "Figured. Though is there actually a vampire prince or something?"

I was surprised when he laughed suddenly. He sighed and said with a smile, "Yeah, but I doubt you'll meet him—ever. Trust me."

I didn't really understand, but I decided I had one more question. "What's the Sorcerer's Crown?"

He was clearly expecting that one. "Yeah, that's the question I was waiting for."

I was madly curious now. "You said something about it being impossible, but Melora said not anymore. Then she looked at me. What do I have to do with this?"

Vince sighed. "I'm not really sure how you or the Sorcerer's Crown ties into all this, but I do know what the Sorcerer's Crown is."

VINCE

I walked forward toward StarLight Hills, though my eyes could only see darkness. I followed the sound of Jason's footfalls as I told him of the Sorcerer's Crown.

"A very long time ago, early in the King of Night's reign, there was a mortal like you who came to our world. He was brave and clever, which made it easy for him to stay alive in our realm. He stayed in our realm and learned our secrets, including magic. He was the first and only mortal to ever learn magic, but that wasn't all. Not only did he learn magic, but he mastered it! He was the greatest of all in his time. He became well-known in our realm as the Sorcerer."

I turned in Jason's direction. "Now understand, you mortals believe sorcerers are another kind of wizard or warlock, but the truth is, there was only ever one sorcerer. It was simply the name he gave himself. He was one of the greatest. He even allied with the King of Night and the prince of that time.

"However, that much power, in a being not meant for it, started to overwhelm him. He started to want more power. He wanted more, to a point that he became obsessed. He was dead set on it! He quickly became a power-hungry madman! Before he could bring any more harm, the King of Night and the prince worked together to seal the Sorcerer's magic into a crown and slay the mortal. The prince locked the crown away where no one could ever get it, though it wasn't really necessary. You see, no night creature could use it. That's why I said it was impossible. Though what changed and what it has to do with you is beyond me."

Jason was silent, but I could hear his breathing and footfalls. He was deep in thought. I wondered what he was thinking, but then he spoke up. "Where are we headed again?"

I was surprised that he jumped completely off subject, but I answered, "StarLight Hills. Why?"

He replied, "Would our destination be a really large mansion on a hill?"

I grinned. "Yeah, that would be it. Phantom Mansion, home to the Fawx family."

I followed Jason's footfalls up a low hill. It was more of a slope, really. Soon he stopped at what I could tell was the front door. I was incredibly familiar with this house.

After all, I just about lived there.

JASON

I pushed the doorbell of the very beautiful mansion. The mansion was black and violet, which seemed perfect for its name—Phantom Mansion. I let Vince stand in front just in case the family reacted badly to seeing a mortal at their door.

Vince rang the bell again, and the door opened to reveal a young man about our age, with long black hair pulled back in a ribbon and eyes like shiny sky-blue diamonds. He may have been our age, but he was dressed like a noble's son, in fancy yet casual clothing. His eyes immediately landed on Vince, and he growled, quickly reminding me of Jamal. "Oh, it's you."

Vince grinned. "Nice to hear your voice, Michael."

Michael grunted at him and walked away, letting us walk in. I was amazed by the house. I had never been in such an amazing house before. Everything was white and gold and elegant beyond compare. It was definitely the home of a very rich family. Though Michael's clothes told me that too.

Then I saw others in the living room as I followed Vince over. Michael sat in an armchair and said, "The vampire's back." I could tell he was obviously a werewolf by how he didn't like Vince so much, though he looked completely human. Well, now I could see why people believed werewolves were so handsome, though I still wondered why Jamal had been more wolf-looking.

A woman who looked to be in her forties looked over at us and smiled. She had black hair in a long braid over her shoulder, though there were streaks of white hair too, making her hair look reminiscent of a bride of Frankenstein. She stood up, which showed how very tall she was, and took Vince's hands. "Welcome back, Vince."

He smiled back, staring past her. "Glad to be back. Sorry I've been gone so long."

She sighed, a worried smile on her kind face. "Yes, after you disappeared, I started to worry about you. It was Fen who told me not to worry."

I was surprised. She spoke to Vince as if he were her own son. I started to wonder.

Then the woman lifted his face to hers gently, seeing as she was a good head taller than him. "My dear, what ever happened to your eyes?" At this, Michael glanced up over the book he was reading.

Vince smiled. "Yeah, a little accident, but it's no big deal. After all these years, the sun finally got me."

She seemed relieved by his optimism. "Well, I'm sure Rose could come up with something."

She called for Rose, but Vince spoke up. "Don't bother, Veil. Witch's magic would only do something worse to me. That includes Rose's magic."

THE DARK EXISTENCE

Then a woman walked in. Well, it was more like she waddled in. I had to bite my tongue not to flinch back at the sight. It was a little old woman with a wrinkly face, dark skin like paper, old green eyes, and white hair like a dirty old mop on her head.

She walked over with a toothy smile. "Well, hello there, handsome." Even her voice sounded sloppy and gravelly at the same time.

Vince smiled back. "If it isn't my favorite witch in the world." He held his hands out, and she took them. He smiled at her, though his eyes couldn't fall on her. "How've you been? Miss me?"

Rose smiled. "Never a day I could live without missing you, Vince."

I almost wanted to barf. What the heck was this? Creepiest thing I had ever seen in all my life, that's what.

Vince must have known I would feel that way, as he grinned. "It's not as creepy as it looks. There's more here than meets the eye."

Rose looked at me and raised an old white eyebrow. "Who's this? A mortal?"

He nodded, still holding her hands. "Yeah, that's Jason. He's with me."

She kept looking me over. I felt nervous. An old cougar looking me over was seriously uncomfortable, I promise you.

She gave me a look. "I know what you're thinking. Don't you judge me. It's not my fault I'm like this."

THE SILVER SPARROW

Vince tried to comfort her. "Of course, it's not. Just ignore him. He doesn't understand yet. He's still pretty new."

She turned away from me and sat on the couch, next to Mrs. Veil. Vince spoke as she did. "I need your help, Rose."

Rose sighed calmly. "Would it have to do with your eyes? You know I can't help you there."

He explained patiently, "I know, Rose, but it's not about that. It's about Sethra."

She jumped to her feet. "What? What is she up to this time?"

Vince eased her back down. "Take it easy, Rose. I ran into Sethra during the time I was gone, and she offered me a proposition."

Rose gave him a look. "You didn't accept, did you? You know how dangerous that girl is."

He was about to go on, but then a large black shadow fell on him—literally. I was surprised as the dark shadowlike thing fell over him. Then I heard a voice say, "Ha! I have you this time, boy!"

I could hear Vince's voice coming from inside. "Oh, come on, old man. This is hardly the time! Besides, I can't see you anymore, so I don't stand even a fraction of a chance." The shadow came off and formed into a very regal man. Vince didn't even turn to him as he explained, "As you may now see, I can't see you. And since sight is the only way I know you're even there, I lose anyways."

THE DARK EXISTENCE

The man had black slicked-back hair and eyes like diamonds, just like Michael. He smiled. "I see. Sorry about that then."

Veil said, "Dear, it seems Vince has something to say that may interest you."

The man sat beside her. "Then let's hear it!"

Vince continued as I sat in a second armchair. "You remember Jamal, right? Well, the proposition was, I join her and Jamal to gather enough of our kinds to force the King of Night to give up his crown. What I didn't know was, that was only half of the plan. I learned that Sethra is going to use *the* spell on the mortals on Hallows' Eve night to create an army."

Everyone, including Michael, gasped in shock and horror. Rose was on her feet again. She exclaimed, "Is she mad? This will topple the already tipping balance! Our world is in enough disaster as it is!"

Vince stuffed his hands into his pockets. "I know. That's why we're looking for a way to stop her. Apparently, there's an old book involved that could mean a lot worse for us than just that spell. We already went to the Witching Sisters, but they only had one idea to offer." I watched their faces as Vince turned toward where he had heard Rose's voice. He said, "The Sorcerer's Crown."

There was a quick intake of breath from Rose. I watched her. She immediately looked at me. That's what I was looking for. I said, "Okay, I saw that. Why is it that every time someone mentions the crown, they look at me? What do I have to do with this?"

Fen seemed to only just notice me. "A mortal?"

THE SILVER SPARROW

Vince waved it off. "My friend Jason. I want to know more about this crown and what Jason has to do with it."

Rose gave it some thought before speaking. "Well, you know the legend, right?"

Vince and I nodded.

She sat back down as she continued, "The thing is, the only person who can use the Sorcerer's Crown is a mortal. No night creature can use it, because only someone like the Sorcerer can wield it."

I was surprised. "That's what that was about? Only I can use it?"

She was hesitant. "That's not all. You see, the crown has every pinch of power and magic the Sorcerer once had. Like him, you're a simple mortal. You weren't meant to have power like that, just like he wasn't. Meaning that if you were to use the crown—" She stopped.

I knew what she was saying. "You mean to tell me, if I use the Sorcerer's Crown, I'll become a power-hungry madman too?"

She nodded. "I fear so."

Everyone was quiet.

Vince was the one to break the silence. "Then we'll just find another way. There has to be something else."

I shook my head. "No way. We're going for that crown."

He looked in my direction as if I was already insane. "Do you *want* to die? The King of Night will not hesitate to slay you, and that's if the crown doesn't do it first!"

I felt that weird rush of confidence again. "I want to stop Sethra! We don't have time to find another way! We'll already be lucky if this works at all before Halloween night!"

Rose scoffed. "If you can *find* it. It was the original prince who hid it, and he's long gone! You'll be lucky if the present prince even knows where it is now!"

Vince pondered over it. "What if we went to see him? Do you think we could? Surely he would have to know something about where it is."

Fen shook his head softly. "That's just about impossible without allowance by one of his own. Only those of the Pumpkin Patch can grant entrance to see him anymore. I am a member of the Night Circle, but that's not enough, especially now that there has been trouble between the King of Night and the prince."

I groaned and rubbed my head. "Okay, can someone translate? I didn't get a single thing of what was just said."

Vince explained, "He's simply saying that we'd need to be granted permission to see the prince by one of his own people. He has a group whom he trusts, like his right-hand guys—and girl. The group is called the Pumpkin Patch. Then there's the Night Circle, which Fen is part of, who all serve directly under the King of Night. Though ever since the King of Night started causing the unbalance, the King of

Night and his son haven't been getting along. They say the prince is furious his father didn't hand over the crown like he was supposed to, so they don't talk to each other. That includes the Pumpkin Patch with him. Even though Fen is a higher-up guy, he can't get us to see the prince, because he serves under the King of Night."

I rubbed my head. "Okay, that makes sense. So how can we find someone from the Pumpkin Patch to help us out?"

Fen scratched his little black goatee. "Well, the only one in the Pumpkin Patch I know of is the Grim Reaper, but let's hope that's the last one you ever meet."

I gulped. "The Grim Reaper? He's real too?"

Vince corrected me. "She. The Grim Reaper is a she. She's a pretty important member of the Pumpkin Patch, being the prince's most powerful ally."

I sighed. Why didn't that surprise me? I yawned as I said, "Well, I guess we'll just have to find someone else from the Pumpkin Patch to help us."

Mrs. Veil stood up. "Not tonight. You need to get some rest. Come, Jason. You can share a room with Michael."

Michael quickly spoke up at that. "No! I don't want him in my room!"

Vince grinned. "Relax. He can stay in the attic with me. I think he'd prefer an old attic with me than a bedroom alone with a werewolf."

I grinned nervously. "Actually, Vince is right. I may be pretty okay with this stuff right now, but I'm

THE DARK EXISTENCE

smart enough not to sleep in a room with a werewolf I don't know or trust."

I followed Mrs. Veil upstairs as Vince talked with the others. I couldn't help but feel kind of impressed with myself. I was in a whole new world full of creatures that could kill me, yet I felt like this was the most normal thing to ever happen to me.

Either I was a really amazing guy, or I was seriously stupid.

VINCE

I sat up with a sigh. I could tell by the feel of the day that it was about nine in the morning. The attic had no windows, so I didn't have to worry about the sunlight.

I pulled a small object from my pocket. It was cold in my hand and about the size of a dog tag. I felt along its edges and knew it was shaped like a flat cross with a word engraved on it. *Mortal* was the word engraved, though it was written in symbols only understood by witches. After all, it was Sethra who gave it to me when I joined her.

I pushed my thumb against the words and spoke its name. "*Mortale Indicium*." The translation was "mortal token." I felt the rush of warmth from the token spread out through my body. I stood, knowing the token had done its job. I was in mortal form. Though it didn't change what I was starving for.

I climbed off the hammock hanging across the room and walked over to the stairs. I listened to the sounds bouncing around me as I walked. I climbed down the steps slowly, so as not to fall on my face. Then I immediately sensed Michael nearby.

THE DARK EXISTENCE

I hissed, "Don't you dare, Michael. I swear, you pull something, and I'll kill you." I heard his quick intake of breath, and I grinned. He was probably trying to cause me to trip. I stepped off the stairs, but my foot caught on something and I fell. To my surprise, someone caught me.

I immediately recognized Jason's voice. "You really should be a little more careful."

I stood up with a hiss. "That stupid werewolf. He'd better be gone."

I could hear the amusement in Jason's voice, so I knew he was smiling when he said, "Yeah, he's gone. The second you tripped, he was outta here."

I smirked. "Smart brat."

I walked down the hall and down the next flight of stairs. I was very familiar with the mansion, so it was no trouble for me to get around. I walked into the living room, where I heard Rose and Fen's voices. I could tell from where their voices came that they were sitting together on the couch.

I grinned as I walked over. "I hope you're not hitting on my witch, Fen."

Fen chuckled, but Jason shivered behind me. I knew he still didn't understand.

I sat in the armchair as I said, "You still think I'm hitting on an old witch, don't you?"

I heard him sit in a chair next to me. "Yeah. You said there's more to it, but I don't see it."

I grinned. "That's because that's the point of the curse. You're not supposed to see it."

He was quiet. I knew he still didn't get it.

I chuckled. "Rose isn't an ugly old woman. She's just under a curse. You see, that's why she hates Sethra. Sethra convinced the Witch Mother that everyone saw Rose as more beautiful and powerful than her, so she got jealous and put the curse on Rose. Now no one can see her true beauty."

Jason sounded surprised. "So she's actually a beautiful young witch that compares to even the leader of all witches?"

I nodded. Then I grinned. "Wait, how'd you know the Witch Mother is leader of all witches?"

I heard him smirk. "Well, duh! She's the *Witch Mother*! Sorta obvious, even for me."

I laughed. "Yeah, I suppose."

Then someone walked in. I gave a mean grin. "If that's the pup, he'd better stay on his feet so he can run when I go for him." I heard Michael's footsteps hurry to the other side of the room, and I laughed.

Then I heard Fen say, "Okay, I have something that might help you, boys. I got word that one of the Pumpkin Patch lives in a nearby town. His name is Tin. If you go find him, you may be able to talk him into granting you entrance to see the prince."

I nodded thoughtfully. "That helps a lot, Fen. Thanks." I turned in Jason's direction. He hadn't said a word. I could guess what he was thinking. "We don't have to do this, Jason. We could try to find another way."

He said, "No. This is the only option we have now. If we don't hurry to find it, we might not make it in time to stop Sethra."

THE DARK EXISTENCE

I heard Rose say, "He's got a good point. And I'm afraid it's the only thing you can do, especially before Hallows' Eve."

I knew I couldn't argue with that. "All right. Then we'd better head to town and find this Tin guy." I stood up and heard Jason do the same. I grinned at the family. "I guess we'll be going then. Once this is over and done with, we'll try to come back."

I felt a little bummed out that I had to leave them again after I had just gotten back from disappearing on them, but I knew that if I survived this, I would be back.

Who knew? Maybe Jason would make it back with me.

JASON

I followed Vince through the marketplace, trying not to stand out. I wore a hooded cloak that hid my face as we went. Vince said we couldn't risk anyone seeing I was mortal. If anyone did, I'd be as good as dead. I tried to avoid looking at people as I walked by. I saw creatures I would never have imagined before.

He seemed to somehow feel my fright. "Just don't look at them. They won't bother you if you stay close and avoid eye contact."

I didn't mind taking his advice, and I just stared straight ahead.

We were halfway into town when Vince stopped. I looked at him and asked, "What's wrong?" I noticed that several other people stopped too. Everyone who had stopped started looking around.

He looked concerned. "Something's coming. Can't you feel it?"

I didn't feel anything until I noticed the weird thump in the ground. Then there was another thump. And another. There were a few seconds between each thump, like footsteps. Very large and heavy footsteps, from the way the ground was shaking with each step.

THE DARK EXISTENCE

I began to fear what it was as several stalls shook. Everyone knew something was coming now.

Then I saw it. An enormous creature, like a giant Minotaur, was walking toward town. Each step spanned half a mile, meaning it wouldn't take long for it to reach town and start crushing everyone. I wasn't the only one who thought that way; people started running for it. A bunch of people kept bumping Vince and me as we tried to get out of the way.

Vince tried to stay on his feet with my help as people kept knocking us around. "What is it?"

I tried to speak over the crowd. "It looks like a Minotaur, and it's headed this way!"

Suddenly, someone bumped us hard, knocking us apart. I kept getting shoved around as I tried to find Vince. "Vince? Vince, where are you?"

Then someone knocked me to the ground. I had to cover my face and pull myself close, trying not to get trampled. Feet kept kicking me and crushing me in their hurry. I begged that nothing heavy would come through, or I was in serious trouble of getting trampled to death. I hoped Vince was all right. Being blind in a loud crowd like this would be impossible for him.

Then the crowds finally stopped, and I looked up. I gasped in horror. There stood the Minotaur.

He scanned the market. Most of the people were indoors, while others tried to look invisible on the sides of the road, against the buildings. I was one of the only ones out in plain sight. I felt my heart stop as the Minotaur's eyes fell on me. My hood had fallen off in the rush. I managed to sit up, but I couldn't get myself to stand and run.

Then the Minotaur reached down for me. I immediately jumped to my feet and ran, but it was too late, as his hand caught me. I felt light-headed as I was lifted high into the air dangerously fast. Only my arm and head were loose from his grasp.

Soon I was being held up to his face. He snorted hot air at me, and his furry face was covered in sweat. I knew that if I wasn't in such a tight grip, I would have been trembling.

Then the Minotaur turned from town and started off. I could see the town running from me with every enormous step. I tried to get loose, but he only squeezed me tighter, which really hurt.

I called out for Vince, but I knew he couldn't help me. I couldn't even be sure that he didn't need help too. For all I knew, he could be trampled and unconscious on the roadside. I could only hope he was all right. And even if he was, he was blind. He'd be lucky if he could tell what had happened at all. I could only watch the town shrink into the distance.

And just when things had been starting to work out.

VINCE

I groaned and opened my eyes as consciousness came back to me. I groaned again when I couldn't see anything anyway. I managed to pull myself up, though my body was in pain. I held my shoulder and listened around. People were moving around like normal, which told me the Minotaur was gone.

Then someone walked up to me. I felt magic around them, which told me it was a wizard. The wizard spoke in the voice of an older man. "Are you all right, young man?"

I nodded. "Yeah, I'm okay."

Suddenly, something hit me—Jason. I turned to the man. "Have you seen someone? A guy around my age wearing a long hooded cloak? We got separated in the crowds. Do you see him anywhere?"

I felt the man move my face to his, I guess to see that I was blind. He sounded sympathetic. "Poor boy. Well, I did see a boy in a cloak, but he was taken by the Minotaur."

I felt my heart sink. Oh no. He was taken by the Minotaur? Oh, that was really bad. He was dead. That was it. Dead. No one who'd ever been taken had ever come back.

THE SILVER SPARROW

The man clearly saw my worry before saying with a sigh, "I'm sorry, but your friend is gone." I heard him start walking away.

I couldn't let Jason die that easily. I still owed him my life. I spoke up. "Which way did it go?"

I heard the man stop. "Excuse me?"

I repeated myself. "Point me in the direction it went in. I have to go after it." I knew that the man thought I was crazy, but he could also see my determination.

He turned my body around. "It walked in that direction. I'm sure if you keep flying that way, you'll find its cave. It's at the base of a mountain. At a vampire's fastest speed, you should get there by twilight."

I was grateful that he pointed out those details. He understood my feel for the time of day and my vampire speed, and he was using that to help me locate the cave easier without my sight. I smiled. "Thank you. I appreciate it."

I hurried off in the direction he pointed me in. Since it was still day, I wouldn't be able to fly, but the sun would set soon enough. Once it did, I could fly and find Jason. I could only hope he would last until I got there.

JASON

I hit the floor painfully, and the cage door then closed and locked. I sat up with a groan. "Thanks for that."

I dusted myself off and looked around. I was in a small cage within a very large cave. I saw bones all around, some not at all human. I tried to relax and stay calm. There was no point freaking out. Looking out the mouth of the cave, I could see that it was already evening. I couldn't stop wondering if Vince was all right.

I sat by the cage wall and opened my bag, which Mrs. Veil had given me, full of supplies I might need. I really did like that family. It was no surprise why Vince hung out there so much. I dug around in it for something to eat.

Suddenly, I jumped as I heard a meow. I looked to see a black cat with big silver eyes. Its right ear and left front paw were white. I noticed it look at my bag, then at me. I sighed and pulled out a ham, lettuce, and cheese sandwich. I ripped it in half and set the one half on the floor for the cat. It quickly hopped over and ate it.

I leaned back against the wall. "I don't usually care for animals, but you must have been here a while." I looked around the room. "Well, from the looks of things, I won't need all this food for long,

THE SILVER SPARROW

so I don't mind sharing." I sighed sadly, starting to feel the weight of my situation. I was going to be a Minotaur's dinner. I closed my eyes and bit my half of the sandwich.

I heard the cat meow again, and I looked over at it. I laughed when I saw that the sandwich was gone, and the cat was sniffing around in my bag. I noticed it was looking at a bottle of milk. I opened it, poured the milk into the large cap of the wide-mouthed bottle, and set it down for the cat. It licked it up hungrily. I drank some out of the bottle and then bit my sandwich again.

I looked at the sky outside; it was getting dark pretty fast. "This sucks. I don't even at least know if Vince is okay. I'm one lousy partner to have. First, Benji dies, though technically that wasn't my fault, and now Vince is out there, blind and alone. Now there's no way anyone will be able to stop Sethra and Jamal either. Everyone I know is gonna be turned into night creatures. Maybe even David! Who knows how many people that spell will change?"

Suddenly, the cat choked. I looked over to see it shake itself and look at me. I was surprised by the look in its eyes. It looked almost... human.

I was shocked when it spoke in a guy's voice, maybe around my age. "What did you say?"

I was silent. I could only stare at it.

The cat walked over to me and asked again, "What did you say just now?"

I stammered, "I-I said Sethra and Jamal were going to turn all those people into night creatures because now I can't stop them."

THE DARK EXISTENCE

The cat rubbed his chin with his paw. "Well, that sounds bad." He glanced at me. "And just why would you be the only person who could stop it? What about this Vince guy you were talking about?"

I was still trying to wrap my head around a talking cat. "Well, for one, he's blind, and another, he's not mortal."

The cat was surprised. "You're mortal?"

I nodded. "Jason Conner. I met Vince, who's a vampire, a week ago. We sorta ended up in the middle of a crazy witch's plans to turn mortals into night creatures and use them for an army against the King of Night."

He looked horrified. "What? Are you serious?"

I nodded again. "We were gonna use the Sorcerer's Crown to stop her, but now I'm stuck here. Can't do anything if I'm eaten by a Minotaur. In fact, we were in town looking for someone from the Pumpkin Patch to help us meet with the prince so he could tell us where the crown is."

The cat pondered over it carefully. "I see."

Just then, the Minotaur came back and stood over us in the cage. The cat gasped. "Uh-oh. Dinnertime."

I got to my feet as the Minotaur opened the cage. I ran from his enormous hand. He missed and tried again. I jumped out of the way, making him miss again. He grunted angrily as I snatched up the cat and went to the back corner, where his hand could just barely reach in. I pushed up against the wall of the cage as he reached for me. His fingers could only just about brush my clothes as he reached in. His upper arm was too full of muscle to get through the door of the cage, so he really had to reach to get me. I pressed back as far as I possibly could with the cat on my shoulder.

The cat said, "I fear it won't be long before he gets smart and shakes us out. Minotaurs are rather slow, so I'd guess we'll be lucky if we get an hour before he looks for another way. Once he does, we're both doomed."

I knew he was right, but there was nothing I could do. I felt the Minotaur's middle finger brush my stomach, which told me he still stood a chance at getting us even now. I closed my eyes and tried to think of ways to get out without being eaten.

Then I heard a loud roar from the Minotaur. I watched as it pulled its hand out and looked around. I gasped as I noticed the small thing flying around its head. It was Vince as his vampire self since it was now dark out.

I felt so much relief. "Vince!"

Vince smiled at the sound of my voice. "So you're still alive! That's a relief!" He ducked as the Minotaur tried to swat him out of the air. I knew he could easily hear those large hands coming and dodge them.

The cat hopped off my shoulder and hurried for the open door. "Come on!"

I ran after him and followed him out of the top of the cage. Once I was on top, I stepped carefully along the cage toward the edge. When I reached the

THE DARK EXISTENCE

edge of the cage, I climbed down, with the cat on my shoulder again. Upon reaching the floor, I looked up at Vince, who was still keeping the Minotaur busy.

I cupped my mouth with my hands and yelled up to him, "Come on, Vince! Let's get out of here!"

He agreed and flew my way, dodging another swat of the Minotaur's hand. He flew down, grabbed me just after I picked up the cat, and flew us quickly out of the cave. I looked back to see the Minotaur coming after us.

The cat looked ahead from where he sat in my arms. "Head to your left! We can lose him over the lake!"

Vince did just that and flew out over a beautiful lake that sparkled under the crescent moon and the stars in the sky. I could see that we were much faster than the Minotaur, and it knew that. It slowed down and roared at us. I sighed with relief. It was giving up.

I knew I spoke too soon when it picked up a rock and threw it at us. The rock flew after us, catching up fast. I gasped, "Vince, look out!" Vince couldn't do anything before the rock knocked us out of the air and into the water.

I hit the water and felt a sting in my arm from the impact of the rock. I could barely move it as I tried to swim for the surface. I managed to break the surface and get a deep breath of air. Just then, the cat's little head popped up. It shook its head. "Ow."

Then I realized Vince was nowhere in sight. That's when I remembered. He was blind, meaning he couldn't swim anymore.

I took a deep breath and ducked back underwater and looked around for him. The water was foggy, making it almost impossible to see anything. I began to panic. Where was he? How far could he have sunk already?

I swam forward, toward where the cat had come up. I hoped that Vince, being a vampire, couldn't drown easily either. He had managed to live after not breathing for quite a while before, so I could only hope he could do the same underwater. Then I noticed movement below me. I felt my lungs begin to hurt as I swam for it. I reached out and felt cloth.

I grabbed it and swam upward, my lungs screaming for air. I broke the surface and lifted Vince up. He gasped for air as his head came up. I felt incredible relief to see that I had found him.

He groaned in clear irritation. "That was awful. I'd never been so lost and desperate before. I hated it."

I laughed in spite of myself, just happy that we were alive.

Vince seemed to understand. He sighed. "Well, we're all in one piece, so I guess it's no big deal."

The cat swam up to us. I was impressed with his swimming ability. He said, "Well, that was sudden. Everyone okay?"

I nodded. "Yeah, we're okay. You?"

He looked around as he replied, "Peachy."

Vince spoke up. "Okay, who's the new guy? New friend of yours, Jason? I didn't even feel the weight of another person when I was flying."

THE DARK EXISTENCE

I smiled. "Yeah, that's because he's a cat."

Vince blinked. "A cat?"

I laughed as I looked at the black cat. "Yeah, we were cellmates."

Vince spoke, a little confused. "Uh, Jason, talking cats aren't normal. Not even in the Hallows Realm do ordinary cats speak."

The cat laughed. "Well, duh, because I'm not an ordinary cat. I'm actually a vampire, but it's a long story. If you can still fly, we should get going. We can talk more on the way."

Vince released his wings and flew up above the water, though I was sure he was worn out and aching from the impact of the rock. He lifted me up by my hands, and the cat hopped into the hood of my cloak. Vince flew off in the direction the cat pointed out.

I smiled at the cat, who peeked over my shoulder from my hood. "So what's your name, cat?"

The cat watched the lake below as he answered, "It's Tamarr. I was cursed by the King of Night years ago for not cooperating with him. He wanted me to give him information given to me and the others by Prince Jack. I refused, and he punished me."

Vince was surprised. "Prince Jack? You've met with Prince Jack-O'-Lantern?"

Why didn't that surprise me? Prince Jack-O'-Lantern? Figures.

Tamarr nodded. "Yep. You see, I am of the Pumpkin Patch."

He showed off his tail, which had a ring on it. The ring was a simple gold band with a pumpkin engraved and painted on it, and four little ruby pieces around the rest of it. I figured it was proof that he was part of the Pumpkin Patch.

Vince looked confused. "Wait, I thought the guy who lived in town was named Tin."

Tamarr smiled. "He is, but I don't live in town. In fact, I'm having us go to my home across the lake. Since I became a cat, I've started living somewhere new. No one knows me very well since I'm stuck as a cat, and most believe the King of Night had killed me. I liked the silence and the lack of hungry werewolves, so I made a new life for myself. Only the others of the Pumpkin Patch and the prince know that's where I live. And now you both will know too."

Vince was suspicious. "How come you're letting us know all this? If only the Pumpkin Patch knows, then why are you telling us?"

He smiled up at Vince. "Because you need my help. And after all, you both did save me, so I owe you my life. The least I can do is trust you. And I must take you to see Prince Jack-O'-Lantern right away."

Vince was about to ask why, but I spoke up. "I told him everything in the cage."

Vince understood. "Oh. Well, I guess at least we can go see him now."

I nodded. "Yeah. We got pretty lucky."

Tamarr grinned confidently. "There's no such thing as luck here, Jason—only fate."

Tamarr

I hopped up on the windowsill of the neat little shack I called home. The two new guys, Vince and Jason, walked in through the door. We were on a hill across the lake, where it was quiet and peaceful, just the way I liked it. I rubbed my ear to dry out the dampness still in my fur. I shook out my fur as the boys looked around.

Jason smirked. "Nice place."

Vince kicked his foot into a chair accidentally. "Yeah, if you like cramped places."

Jason pulled out a chair, and Vince sat down so as not to trip over anything else. I was pretty curious how a vampire like him had ended up blind. Obviously, he hadn't always been blind. In fact, it seemed quite recent.

I hopped over onto the table and lifted the lid off a large jar of shortbread cookies with my nose and another jar of milk. I couldn't open bottles, containers, or boxes as a cat, so Prince Jack had a few of my comrades in the Pumpkin Patch help me out by putting food and drinks out where I could reach them. I was grateful for the help. It made the curse all the easier to live with.

THE SILVER SPARROW

I pulled a cookie out and groaned when I saw that it was stale and covered in dust. Obviously, Krank hadn't done anything at the house since I was caught by that Minotaur. He probably saw I wasn't home and decided to just leave. What a jerk.

Jason spoke as he sat in another chair. "So how can you help us meet with Prince Jack-O'-Lantern here?"

I sighed, a bit annoyed now. "I can't fly anymore, and I'm sure your friend's exhausted. So I'll have to call on someone else to take us to the castle." I pushed the cookie away and sniffed the milk. I recoiled at the smell of spoiled milk.

Vince must have been a vampire of incredibly strong senses. He somehow noticed my recoil. "What's wrong?"

I was highly impressed, but I groaned. "That idiot Krank didn't do anything while I was gone. Now I'm starving, and everything I have to eat or drink is stale or spoiled."

Jason smirked as he watched me. "I was wondering how you ate and drank now that you're a cat. I thought maybe you just worked it out like a cat."

I laughed. "No way. I'm still a civilized vampire. Some comrades of mine from the Pumpkin Patch set that up for me. Thanks to Prince Jack, someone from the Pumpkin Patch comes and has food and milk laid out so I can actually use it." I glanced at the milk and cookies. "Though not all of them are as helpful as they could be." I hopped back onto the counter.

THE DARK EXISTENCE

"Maybe Reaper can lend us a hand with seeing Prince Jack."

Jason stood up and walked over to one of the cabinets. "And while we wait, I'll see if there's anything else around that's still edible."

I smiled. "Sounds good." I hopped onto the windowsill and raised my tail with the pumpkin ring up high. The ring began to glow a soft orange as it signaled to Reaper. After a moment, the glow turned to gold. I smiled. She got my signal and was on her way.

I hopped back down on the counter, where Jason was pouring water into a dish. He even popped open a pack of crackers that were still fresh from the sealed packet.

My stomach growled as I walked over. "Looks like there's some stuff left over from a couple of other times. Thank goodness."

Jason looked at me as he ate a cracker and asked, "Just how long were you caught by that Minotaur?"

Vince smirked. "And how did an enormous Minotaur catch a cat?"

It was an unfortunate tale, to be honest. "Well, that's a funny story. See, I was headed to town when the Minotaur showed up. So as not to be crushed under his big feet, I hid in a passerby's bag. Unfortunately, that same guy got caught and was taken to the cave. I must have hit my head while in that bag because by the time I got out of the bag, I was in the cage—alone, might I add."

Jason caught my drift and gave a look of disgust.

THE SILVER SPARROW

I ate a cracker as I continued. "So I was stuck there, if I had to assume, about four days."

He was surprised. "Four days? I could barely stand one evening."

I shrugged as I licked up the water. "Well, honestly, I think being a cat helped with that."

Then there was a sudden gust of wind outside.

I grinned. "Oh, good. She's here." I turned to the door and said, "You can come in, Reaper."

Vince gulped in his chair. "Wait, Reaper wouldn't happen to be—"

Then the door opened, and lightning struck outside behind her. She was as dark and deadly as ever. Her cocoa skin and short black hair were the only things about her that reminded you of who she really was. Her deep-red eyes were without any feeling, and her clothes were long and black. She wore a black fedora and a long black leather coat over simpler black clothing. A large scythe was strapped to her back, while her hands were in her pockets. She walked in, her thick boots thudding against the wood floor.

The door closed behind her on its own as she looked in our direction. Jason was clearly intimidated by her dark energy, as he seemed to shrink back. Vince didn't even have to see to look a bit nervous in his chair.

I just smiled, completely used to her. "Greetings, Grim Reaper."

That's right. She was the current Grim Reaper.

She spoke in a soft, mysterious yet strict voice. "Greetings, Tamarr. I see you've returned. His Highness was beginning to worry."

I smiled. That was Prince Jack for you. "I'm fine. Starving, but fine," I replied.

Reaper's eyes scanned the room in one quick swoop. She, of course, noticed the old cookies, the spoiled milk, and our little scrounging progress.

Her eyes squinted slightly, which I knew meant she was angry. "Krank did not show up?"

I sighed as I finished another cracker. "He probably did, but I wasn't here. So he didn't bother doing anything." I saw the flash of anger in her eyes, but her expression didn't change. I knew Krank was going to be really sorry he didn't just do what he was told.

Reaper was one of Prince Jack's most loyal night creatures, so she was very strict on making sure everyone followed his orders—including the seemingly insignificant job of feeding the cat. After all, after I was cursed for protecting the prince's privacy, Reaper's had a soft spot for me, so even this was a seriously important responsibility in her eyes. That, and she's always loved cats.

I remembered the other reason I had called her. "Oh, Reaper, meet Jason and Vince. They need to go see Prince Jack."

Reaper's expression still didn't change, but I could see the slight rise of her left eyebrow. "Is that so?" She looked them over.

I nodded as I ate another cracker. "Yes, there is a very serious problem they need to discuss with him.

THE SILVER SPARROW

It's urgent. I can't take them all the way to the castle, so I was hoping—"

She finished for me. "That I would take you all?"

I gave her a smile. "Pretty please?"

She sighed. "Very well. I see you trust them, and I trust you."

She grabbed her scythe and lifted it up high, then brought it down, cutting the air with a quick slice. A portal appeared, like she had sliced open the very air. I loved when she did that.

She turned to us. "Let's go."

I didn't want to leave before I got a chance to tame the hunger in my gut, but she said, "I'll have something prepared for you at the castle. Krank still owes you a meal." I grinned and hopped off the counter to the floor.

Reaper stepped through the portal as Vince stood up and said to Jason, "She made a portal, didn't she?"

Jason took his wrist and stepped through the portal. I followed right after them. This was going to be an interesting trip.

JASON

I stepped out of the portal into a large stone room. It was huge and decorated with what looked like royal banners on the walls and other such fancy things, so I assumed it was a castle. Though it was also deathly quiet. Tamarr stepped out behind Vince and me, then the portal closed.

The Grim Reaper turned back to us and said, "Follow me." She started walking down a connecting hallway. I let go of Vince's wrist since the sound of our footsteps was easy to hear in the empty stone room. We followed her down the hall in silence.

Tamarr climbed up on me and hopped up on my shoulder, which I was coming to like. "So you've been enjoying your time in the Hallows Realm so far?"

I smiled back at him. "Yeah, kinda. Some of the night creatures around here still creep me out, but I've met a few nice people since coming here. So that kinda makes up for it."

Tamarr chuckled. "Yeah, makes sense. Some of us can be pretty creepy." He glanced at the Grim Reaper up ahead. "What about Reaper? She scare you?"

I looked at her. "Honestly? Not really. She seems pretty cool."

He grinned. "Is that right? Well, I agree 100 percent." He grinned wider. "You should see her when she isn't the Grim Reaper."

I was surprised. "When she isn't the Grim Reaper? What do you mean?"

He could only grin before we entered the next room.

It was a large stone throne room with a floor of dirt and grass around the stone landing a couple of steps up. It was like a small indoor field, while black banners hung on the stone walls.

On the banners was a big orange pumpkin with a scythe crossing behind it. Actual pumpkins were growing all around the field floor. Where a throne would have been on the landing, there instead sat a stone pedestal big enough to sit on and a large full-length mirror facing it a bit, to its left. On the pedestal was a pumpkin the size of a head.

I was amazed. I had never seen such an amazing room. We followed Reaper up to the landing. She had us stop and went to stand beside the pedestal.

Tamarr smiled as he did the talking. "Boys, meet Prince Jack-O'-Lantern."

I blinked at the pumpkin. "But it's a pumpkin."

Vince nudged me in the ribcage with his elbow. "He *is* the pumpkin, Jason."

I just stared at the pumpkin. "It's not even a jack-o'-lantern, just an average pumpkin. I could

THE DARK EXISTENCE

understand a talking jack-o'-lantern, but this seems weird, even for this realm."

He nudged me again, but harder. "Watch it, man. Pumpkin or not, he's still the prince." He seemed a bit nervous. "And unless you want the Grim Reaper to remind you of your place, I suggest you behave."

I held my hands up in surrender. "Okay, okay, sorry. Still just getting the hang of things." I even gave the pumpkin a little bow as I said, "I apologize, Your Highness."

Then something surprising happened. Shadows started to pour out from under the pumpkin, raising it into the air. The shadows then formed into an actual body, and the pumpkin slowly morphed and changed color. Black hair grew out the top, while the texture of the pumpkin became smooth and soft.

Before I knew it, a guy with a completely pitch-black body was sitting before me on the pedestal. He looked somewhat older than me, but I really couldn't be sure. He had a look to him that seemed ageless. He had black hair that hung in his face and halfway to his shoulders. And his eyes were like nothing I had ever seen before. The irises and pupils were replaced by what looked like balls of light. They were white at the center, turning yellow as it spread outward, then orange along the edges.

He smiled and spoke with a voice that sounded something like a dark angel, gentle yet full of power and authority. "Welcome, Jason Conner."

My jaw dropped. "No way."

Vince grinned. "Told you."

Tamarr hopped off my shoulder and scampered up the landing and onto the guy's lap. The guy smiled at the cat. "I see you've returned, Tamarr. I'm glad to see you're well."

Tamarr hopped onto his shoulder. "Yeah, I'm fine. Though I could really use something to eat now."

Reaper thumped the end of her scythe on the floor. "Krank!"

Then someone hurried in. He was a wide man with a bald head. He looked cranky and tough, with little horns coming up from the top of his head and a huge underbite that revealed crooked teeth. "Yes, Grim Reaper?"

She glared at him. "You dare avoid your tasks?"

The prince raised an eyebrow. "Now what would this be about?"

He clearly knew, but he was letting Krank admit it himself. Krank looked nervous. Clearly, this was their respected prince. He just had that impact on those below him that made a person feel ashamed to disappoint him.

Krank fell on his knees. "Please forgive me, Your Highness. I didn't see the cat there, and I didn't bother to look. I figured it was just a stupid cat. I meant no disrespect toward you, my prince."

Tamarr looked very much insulted.

Prince Jack spoke softly. "I'll take your word for it, but from now on, I'd like my orders to be carried out thoroughly." He scratched behind Tamarr's ear.

THE DARK EXISTENCE

"Tamarr is one of us and should be treated as such. His condition is because of his loyalty, and I believe that should be treated with the highest respect, no matter the shape or form."

Krank bowed so low his bald head touched the floor. "Yes, Your Highness. Of course."

Prince Jack waved him away. "You may go now. I would like you to bring something for our guests."

Krank scrambled to his feet. "Yes, my prince!" With that, he hurried off.

I was amazed. Why couldn't all rulers and world leaders be that kind and understanding?

Prince Jack smiled. "He's troublesome but harmless."

Tamarr scoffed. "Tell that to my growling stomach and my injured pride as a vampire. A stupid cat? Really?"

Prince Jack looked at him and asked, "Just where were you, Tamarr?"

He hesitated to answer, but then he sighed. "Trapped by a Minotaur. Been trapped for the last four days. It's thanks to him I'm here." He pointed at me with his tail.

I felt my face grow warm as their attention fell on me. I looked at Prince Jack as he looked at me. For the strangest reason, he seemed awfully familiar to me.

Then Krank returned with trays of food. Vines grew from the ground and formed themselves into a decent table. He set the tray down, gave a low bow, and then left. Prince Jack waved a hand toward the table. "Help yourselves."

Tamarr grinned. "Don't mind if we do!"

He hopped down and onto the table, then started eating right away. Even Vince took some food.

I didn't pay much attention to the food. I was still set on Prince Jack. I even found myself saying, "Have we met before?"

Prince Jack's eyebrow rose curiously.

Vince scoffed. "Kid, there is no way in any world that you could have met Prince Jack before. He's the prince! He's probably never even gone to your world—at least, not within only seventeen years of now."

I knew he was probably right, but I still felt something when I looked at Prince Jack—something familiar and important.

Prince Jack said, "So what brings you two here? Must be something important if Tamarr granted you entrance here."

Reaper crossed her arms. "Even I do not know their business yet, but Tamarr was insistent."

Tamarr turned to me. "Tell him everything you told me."

Well, what was one more retelling? "There's a witch named Sethra who wants to create an army to overthrow the King of Night. She plans to use *the* spell."

Prince Jack didn't understand. "*The* spell? What spell?"

THE DARK EXISTENCE

I honestly didn't know, but I hoped he would understand like everyone else had when Vince said it. "You know, *the* spell."

The prince still wasn't getting it.

Vince grinned. "He means *the* spell, Your Highness."

Suddenly, Prince Jack jumped to his feet. "What?"

I felt a little annoyed. How come he understood when Vince said it? He didn't say it any differently than I did!

The prince looked grim as he thought to himself silently. Tamarr finished eating and made his way back up to Jack's shoulder. He spoke as his tail brushed against Prince Jack's ear. "Yeah, and if that's not enough, they wanna find the Sorcerer's Crown."

Prince Jack looked utterly shocked. Then he looked at us. "Are you serious?"

I didn't feel as confident under his gaze. "The witches all agree the Sorcerer's Crown may be the only way to stop Sethra."

Jack looked at me as if I was insane, which I was starting to believe I was. He walked up to me. "Do you even know what it is? What it will do to you?" He stopped face-to-face with me, Tamarr still on his shoulders. I could only look into those eyes as he said, "The Sorcerer's Crown is a weapon. Its sole purpose is to take over the King of Night—to take over all power! It will use any and every single innocent person who puts it on to do it. Life means nothing compared to power in the mind of those who possess the Sorcerer's Crown, just as he once did. That crown was created to seal away the evil that lived and grew in that mortal's heart, and it is now my duty to see to it that it can never be released again."

He gave me a grim look. "Do not think you are the first to believe he is capable of controlling that kind of power. Over the decades, other mortals found their way into our world and tried to use the crown, but they easily fell to it. Even once, my own life was nearly taken for power by the fool who possessed the crown. And in truth, I believed he could overcome its madness." His grim expression looked pained at the memory. "I was severely wrong."

I felt my blood run cold with every word he said. Maybe I really was getting in over my head. Maybe I was just as foolish as the others. Jack turned from me, pondering on his own words in silence.

I could only stare at the soil under my feet. I could see a young pumpkin and a smaller one sitting together. I then thought of my little brother, David. He looked a lot like me, with his short blond hair and big blue eyes. He even had this really cheesy smile that always made people laugh, including me.

I thought about what would happen if Sethra's plan worked, how everyone I knew would become night creatures, including David, who was only ten. That little kid I always watched out for becoming something like a werewolf or a Minotaur? I clenched my fists. I couldn't let that happen.

Vince seemed to feel my determination, as he turned in my direction curiously.

THE DARK EXISTENCE

I spoke up. "I don't care."

Jack turned back to me, his expression somewhere between bored and deep in thought.

I looked at him, more determined than before. "I don't care. I don't care what happens to me. I won't let Sethra hurt my little brother or anyone else."

Jack raised an eyebrow. "Is that so?"

I clenched my fists tighter. "I'll die a thousand deaths before I let Sethra get away with her plans. Not just my world will suffer if she wins. Yours will too."

Jack looked curious. So did Tamarr, who tilted his little head.

I felt courage grow in me a little. "I may die, but not before I win this fight. I will stop Sethra, even at the cost of my own life. That's a sacrifice I'm willing to make."

Jack surprised me by getting angry at me. "You are such a child!"

I recoiled at his sudden outburst.

His eyes reddened in color, reminding me of fire. "You think you're the only one who would be making a sacrifice if you take that crown? You say that's a sacrifice you're willing to make! What about everyone else, huh? What about the people you hurt when you put that crown on? When the crown takes over, you will not just hurt Sethra—you'll kill her and everyone else you cross! When you put on that crown, you're not just sacrificing your own life. You're sacrificing the lives of many others! Your friend here would be one of the first!"

I was shocked, but I glanced at Vince, who looked a little worried.

Jack stood erect. "Don't be another fool, Jason. No one's life is worth that."

He turned and walked back up onto the landing, where Reaper still stood by his pedestal. I felt ashamed and embarrassed. I felt like the biggest idiot who'd ever lived. But I said softly, "But are all those lives worth letting Sethra win?"

Jack stopped before his pedestal, but he didn't look back. Tamarr looked sympathetic, though I couldn't tell if it was for me or Jack.

I continued, staring at the ground. "That's a lot of people. I know this is an incredible risk, but it'll be even worse if she wins. Not just all those people, but also all of the Hallows Realm. Rose said the balance would topple if her plan succeeds, and there's no saying it can ever be fixed. One way or another, someone, if not many more, will get hurt. Maybe even killed. So which is more worth the risk?" I felt the fire in my heart as I said, "You tell me, Prince Jack."

The room was silent.

I looked up and was surprised by the sorrow in Jack's eyes as he watched me. "I don't know." He sat on his pedestal as he continued. "I fear I've been without knowing a long time now. Ever since my father caused the unbalance, nothing seems to make sense. Before, I knew everything. I could make the right choices and protect everyone to the best of my ability. But now…"

THE DARK EXISTENCE

He closed his eyes and pinched the bridge of his nose. "Now I can't even protect my Pumpkin Patch. Tamarr was taken by a Minotaur for four days, and I could do absolutely nothing about it. I didn't even know where he was or what had happened to him. At one time, I started to fear it was my father's doing. Though I suppose it still is. I can no longer do my job as the Pumpkin Prince. My power is no longer under my control because of the unbalance, meaning I can't keep the peace in this realm. Everyone's trust in me is fading. I can't seem to do any of the things they need of me. Now both our realm and yours are in horrifying danger, and I don't know what to do about it."

I heard the pain and misery in his voice. He ran his hand through his hair and said with a defeated sigh, "And now I see you about to sacrifice your life to fix things, and I can't seem to find a way to prevent it. No one should have to sacrifice themselves like that. It's not right, and it's not fair. You're just a kid. You've done nothing wrong to deserve that."

I felt deeply sad for Jack. He was more than any prince I could ever have imagined. He didn't want anyone to get hurt, even me. And to see that he'd have to let someone possibly die to fix what he couldn't, it hurt him more than anything—to know that no matter what he did, he couldn't do anything. I could feel his agony at the thought.

I walked up to him on the landing and said, "I know you wanna fix things. You don't want any more pain for anyone. I understand that, but you could help me."

He looked at me. His pain seemed emphasized by his eyes, which seemed to have become paler than they originally were. They even seemed to be a shade of blue.

He sighed and spoke very softly. "And how is that?"

Trying to be positive, I said, "Help us find the crown. Help me use it right. Help me stay, you know, me. I know you can."

He only watched me.

I knew, as I looked in his eyes, that I was right about knowing him. He was unbelievably familiar to me. But how? Could he be reminding me of someone I knew? If so, then who?

He seemed to ponder the thought deeply and thoroughly as he looked at me. Then he glanced at his mirror. I glanced too and saw us in its reflection. But something was wrong with it.

I was younger. Just a kid. And Jack, he was different too. Before I could figure out what made him different, I blinked, and it was back to normal. It was just him and me standing there, looking into the mirror.

Jack seemed to be looking deeply into it as if it showed him something I couldn't see. I started to wonder if he saw what I saw, but I figured he probably didn't.

Then he finally spoke. "Very well."

I looked at him.

THE DARK EXISTENCE

He looked at me, looking weak, as if he had just finished the battle that had been raging within him. "The Sorcerer's Crown is in the North. There you will find another of my Pumpkin Patch, whom I entrusted to hide the crown. He is a powerful wizard called Ashura. He can help you."

I could hear the pain in his voice as he told me this. I knew he really hated the idea of sending me after the crown. I hated to see him so sad. "I know this is a hard choice for you to make, but I won't let you down." I smiled, in hopes of cheering him up. "Thank you, Jack."

Vince spoke up from the bottom of the landing. "It's *Prince* Jack, Jason."

I realized I had called him just Jack. "Oh, sorry, Prince Jack."

Jack smiled, which I was a bit relieved to see. "I'm not your prince, Jason, so there is no need to treat me as such. You can just call me Jack."

I actually rather liked it when he smiled, strangely enough. "Sure."

Vince spoke up again. "So we head to the North and find a wizard named Ashura? Wait, why is a wizard from the North part of your Pumpkin Patch? The North is outside of your reign here in the Night Kingdom, so he doesn't serve you or the King of Night."

Jack shook his head softly. "No, he doesn't, but he is a very dear friend of mine, one of my most trusted allies."

I could understand that. "Okay. Then I guess we will go find Ashura. How do we get to him?"

Jack looked over at the Grim Reaper. "Reaper can give you a portal to the North. Though because of the magical field he has placed around his home, she won't be able to place you right there. You'll have to make your way to him. I'll contact him to let him know you're looking for him." He sighed, looking a little worried. "Hopefully, Oz or Sid can collect you before anyone else can."

I asked curiously, "What do you mean? Is there someone to be careful of there?"

Vince scoffed. "Are you kidding? This is the North we're talking about, Jason—the land of wizarding kind! The North is split up into territories among the many powerful wizards and witches who live there, and some of them are *very* territorial. If we wander into the territory of a not-so-nice wizard or witch, we're in big trouble."

Reaper walked off the landing and cut us a portal with her scythe. "I will do my best to get you as close as I can, but also keep you out of the wrong territories. I would advise staying put and lying low until Sir Ashura can collect you."

Jack nodded, still looking worried. "That would be wise."

I smiled, trying to ease his worries. "Don't worry, Jack. We'll be careful."

Jack didn't seem assured as I led Vince over to the portal. Then he said, "Tamarr, go with them. I

THE DARK EXISTENCE

need to know someone I trust can watch them for me." He glanced at the cat still on his shoulder.

Tamarr gave him a reassuring smile. "If it'll make you feel better."

He hopped down and hurried over to us. I let him hop up on my shoulder. Jack looked just a little less worried as we walked up to the portal.

Before I could walk into the portal, Jack spoke once more. "Jason, one last thing."

I turned back to him. "Yes?"

He smiled softly. "Promise me, no matter what happens, you'll remember what's most important."

I didn't understand what he meant by that, but I smiled. "I promise."

He smiled back, finally seeming a little more reassured.

I gave him a confident grin. "We'll be fine. You'll see."

With that, I stepped through the portal.

JASON

I stepped out of the portal, only to be greeted by freezing cold winds. I immediately held myself tightly against the cold. "Oh gosh, what the heck?"

Tamarr noticed and grinned as he hopped up on my shoulders, getting the snow from his paws on my clothes. "Whoops. Probably should have gotten you something warm to wear first. My bad."

I groaned, and I looked over to see snow everywhere. "Let me guess. You're not cold 'cause you're technically still a vampire?"

Tamarr could only grin, a bit embarrassed. "Good guess. Jack is never bothered by the cold either, so we forget others are, like a mortal kid."

I noticed Vince was already in his mortal form, and the sky was light, though cloudy. We were obviously very far up north. Vince shrugged. "Even in my mortal form, I'm not cold."

I grabbed his wrist. "Lucky for you guys."

With that, we walked down the little hill we were on.

Soon enough, to my utter relief, we found a small town. It was a pretty quiet little town, so I hoped it didn't have any of those wizards Jack had

THE DARK EXISTENCE

warned about. The streets had few people, and most of the windows of the houses were lit, like something off a Christmas card. I was surprised to spot a castle far off outside of town, the street through town leading out to it. I wondered if the wizard running this territory lived there.

We walked into a little shop, and I was extremely grateful to find it was heated. I let Tamarr down and rubbed my hands together to get some feeling back into them. Vince sniffed the air and said, "Smells good in here. We're in a bakery?"

I hadn't even checked. I looked around and found my mouth watering at the sight of all the delicious baked goods around us. It did smell incredible.

Tamarr smiled. "I remember this place. Jack and I have been here once before. That was years ago though, back before all this crap with the King of Night, of course. Poor Jack's been cleaning up his mess ever since it started."

I tried to imagine Jack sitting in this little shop with Tamarr, and I smiled. For some reason, thinking of Jack as just a normal person made me want to smile.

Then an older woman with gray hair in a bun and a wrinkly old smile walked over. "Welcome, strangers. I do hope it's warm enough in here for you."

We turned to her, except Vince, of course.

I smiled. "It is. Thanks."

I was surprised to notice ginger cat ears peeking out from her hair and what looked like the end of a matching cat tail peeking out from under her dress. It figured that she wasn't just an average little old lady.

Tamarr hopped onto my shoulder. "Perhaps you could help us. Would you happen to know where we can find a wizard by the name of Ashura around here?"

The woman was surprised. "Ashura?" She smiled. "Why, yes, in fact, I do. May I ask why you're looking for him?"

I liked this old lady. "Prince Jack sent us to find him. We need his help with something."

The woman said, "Ah, I see. Yes, Prince Jack often has dealings with Ashura." Then she looked a bit concerned. "Though I am surprised you would come to Convile's territory of all places to find Ashura. They have been enemies for generations."

I didn't like the sound of that. "In other words, we're in the territory of the enemy of the wizard we're looking for?"

She nodded.

Tamarr was just as worried as I was, only proving that I was right to be. "Oh, boy. Then we really should get out of here. Ashura won't be able to come find us here. Can you tell us where the end of this guy's territory is, so we can get out of here?"

Before she could answer, Vince gasped. "Uh-oh. We've got company, guys."

At that moment, the door was thrown open, and some guys stormed in. They wore the average soldier uniform for a castle guard, except the colors were blue and white, and though they looked like

THE DARK EXISTENCE

young men, their hair was white. And all four of them were identical, which told me they weren't normal people.

One of the soldiers spoke. "Hand over the Pumpkin Patch cat, by order of Lord Convile."

Tamarr tensed on my shoulder. "Uh-oh."

The woman spoke up, looking angry. "How dare you come barging into my shop like this? You have no right to—" She was interrupted by one of the soldiers shoving her aside to the floor.

I quickly went down to help her. "Are you all right?"

She nodded, but she looked worried as the soldiers surrounded us. I looked to see that they had already managed to grab Vince and now had him pinned to the ground as he continued to fight against them. Leave it to Vince not to go down without a fight, even while blind.

The soldiers pointed their spears at me as I kept Tamarr and the woman behind me. I glared at them. "What could you possibly want with a cat, huh? He can't do anything!"

Another of the soldiers spoke, his voice matching that of the first guy. "Lord Convile will not allow for spies against the King of Night in his territory. Hand it over or suffer the consequences."

I was surprised when Vince managed to throw the soldiers off him and ram into the soldiers pointing their spears at me. I quickly got to my feet while he had them distracted, and I helped the woman up, saying, "Go in the back and lock the door." She nodded and hurried off to the back of the shop. No need for her to get hurt here.

However, before I could try to help Vince, I was surprised to find I couldn't move my feet. I looked down and gasped, finding a thick layer of ice climbing up my legs. I was becoming encased in ice. I was about to call Vince for help, only to find ice quickly climbing his legs too. The soldiers didn't even bother fighting with us now, knowing we were caught.

Tamarr gasped from my shoulder. "Oh no! Jason! Vince!"

I looked over my shoulder at him. "Tamarr, you're the one they're after, so you need to get out of here while you still can!"

He looked at me with worried silver eyes. "I can't just leave you two! Who knows what Convile will do to you?"

I grabbed him and tossed him onto a table by a sliding window. "Don't worry, just go! You can find Ashura for help!"

Tamarr looked unsure about leaving us, but when the soldiers started after him, he quickly managed to pull the window open and hop out just before they could grab him. He got away.

My attention quickly turned to the ice that was now climbing my chest and that had quickly encased my arms. I found myself gasping for breath from the solid cold of it. I looked over to find Vince in the same trouble, looking as worried as I felt. I shut my eyes and managed one last breath before the ice climbed over my face and I was completely encased.

THE DARK EXISTENCE

What happened after that, I honestly don't know. All I knew was the cold. I was freezing and completely unable to move. It was an awful experience, unlike anything I had felt before. I'm sure I blacked out a few times, so I don't even know how long I was like that. I wasn't even sure why I didn't feel like I was suffocating. Maybe this was what it was like for animals who hibernated, the cold slowing my heart and making it so I could go longer without breathing.

Though, at some point, I did feel my lungs start to ache. Whether it was from the piercing cold or lack of air, I wasn't sure. All I knew was that I just wanted it to end.

To my great relief, it finally did. I'm sure I had blacked out again just before I was freed because I found myself coming to while on the floor and gasping for air. I felt my lungs cry out in pain from the cold air around me as I tried to catch my breath. I was sure that if it were any colder, I would be struggling to breathe at all.

As I tried to get my bearings, a voice spoke. "A mortal? Well, isn't this an interesting surprise."

I sat up to find I was sitting in a puddle of water in what looked like a castle throne room made of crystalized ice. The fact that I wasn't sticking to the floor from my wet clothes told me it wasn't actually ice, despite the room feeling cold enough to be.

Vince, just as wet as I was, rushed to my side. "Are you okay, Jason?"

I nodded. "Yeah, I'm fine. I think. Never been frozen like that before."

That's when I noticed we weren't alone. Soldiers stood around the room, and a new figure sat on the icy throne. He was a tall man in long blue-and-white robes, with very long white hair and beady blue eyes. He looked like an old wizard from fairy tales.

He spoke as he watched us. "So there are three spies, hmm? I suppose that makes more sense. I had heard rumors of the cat once having been Prince Jack's spy, but I'm rather surprised he still continues to be even in his tiny cat form. Explains a lot that he would have assistance." He squinted down at me. "Though I find it odd that he would bring a mortal to aid him. What is a mortal even doing in the Hallows Realm?"

I knew better than to tell him the truth, so I decided to play dumb. "I don't really know, sir. All I know is that I was teleported here somehow. Vince and Tamarr were just helping me to not get killed. We're not here to spy on you, sir, I swear."

The old man, whom I assumed was the Convile guy I had been hearing about, rubbed his bearded chin. "Is that so?" He pointed a bony finger at me. "Then why was the portal you came out of one of the Grim Reaper's portals? It can only mean you came from Prince Jack, and I highly doubt the prince would send you here without reason." He gave me a chilling grin. "I know why you're really here. You came to aid that brat Ashura by spying on me. You want to know the King of Night's secrets. I am the most trusted member of the Night Circle, so you were hoping to collect the king's secrets for his rebellious son, weren't you?"

I remembered Fen mentioning the Night Circle and how they served under the king, the way the Pumpkin Patch served Jack.

Convile smirked. "But perhaps we could work something out instead."

Vince looked suspicious of the old wizard. "And what do you mean by that?"

Convile grinned as he stood and crossed his arms behind his back. "I mean there is only one way you two are getting out of this alive, and that's by telling me what Prince Jack is up to. My king would be most grateful for the knowledge of his foolish son."

I also remembered how Fen told us that Jack and the King of Night refused to speak to each other anymore. It didn't come as a surprise to me that the King of Night would want inside information. After all, that was how Tamarr had ended up a cat in the first place.

I glared at the wizard. "Like I'd betray Jack to you or your awful false king."

The wizard looked red in the face with anger as he yelled, "You will not speak of His Majesty that way, you rotten little brat!" He stormed down to us, making Vince and me jump to our feet, only for us to be grabbed from behind by the soldiers.

Convile glared as he stood a full head taller than us. "For that, I will take your friend's life here and now." I felt sick as the wizard stood in front of Vince.

The guards held tightly to me when I tried to stop him. "No! Leave him alone!"

Convile ignored me as he stood before Vince with an evil grin. "Let's see what happens if I remove that token during the day."

Vince paled.

Just then, I heard noise from a nearby room. Convile's hand was at Vince's pocket when he stopped to hear what sounded like blades clashing. "What is that?"

Suddenly, the doors were thrown open, and several guards were thrown to the floor in a heap of unconscious bodies. I was just as surprised as Convile was when two figures walked into the room.

One was a very big, strong guy with medium-toned skin, silver eyes, and green hair with long bangs, the top half of his hair pulled back and the rest hanging to his shoulders. The other figure was a lanky yet tough-looking guy with long violet hair brushed back under a black biker cap with a silver chain, and eyes a mixture of sky blue and purple that seemed to shift around slowly, like a lava lamp. They wore matching black-and-white uniforms with slacks and vests.

I smiled when I noticed the familiar cat on the shorter guy's shoulder. "Tamarr!"

Tamarr saw us and smiled. "Oh, good. We made it." He looked over at Convile and hissed, "Let them go, Convile!"

The big guy smirked. "I'd listen to him, old man. The boss is not happy about how you attacked his niece in her shop. He warned you what he'd have us do with you if you ever harmed her."

I was surprised. The old woman was Ashura's niece?

Convile scoffed. "You think I'm afraid of that brat? This is *my* territory! I will do as I please on it!" He grinned cruelly. "Including kill whoever I see fit!"

The lanky guy looked serious. "Watch it, old man. The boss made it very clear that we were not to hold back on you this time. You hurt his family, you hurt his fellow Pumpkin Patch, and now you're threatening people his closest friend has under his protection. You're in a very dangerous position here, so do yourself a favor and hand them over."

Convile smirked. "I'd love to see you try and stop me." He looked at the other soldiers and commanded, "Kill them!"

The soldiers rushed at the two guys. Tamarr hopped off the one's shoulder as they prepared to fight.

As they fought, Convile turned to me. "Under Jack's protection, hmm?" He walked over to me and looked me in the eye. "Now what could make a mortal like you so important to that rotten prince?"

Vince struggled against the soldiers holding him. "Back off, wizard!"

Suddenly, Convile made a long, thin knife appear and, to my horror, stabbed Vince in the side with it. I gasped as the soldiers let Vince collapse to the floor in pain. "Vince!"

Convile then turned to me, pointing the knife in my face, just under my nose so I could catch the sickening scent of Vince's blood on the blade. He glared at me. "Just who are you, boy?"

I didn't dare answer.

Just then, Tamarr jumped on Convile's back with a loud hissing shriek as he started clawing and biting the old wizard. Convile backed away as he tried to get Tamarr off. I used this opportunity to struggle against the soldiers holding me, who had been temporarily unsure what to do, knocking them aside as I got free. I rushed to Vince, as the soldiers who had been holding him were now busy helping against the two intruders. "Vince! Vince, answer me!"

Vince groaned as he held his side in pain. "I'll be fine. Luckily, he didn't stab me with anything too serious. I'll heal."

I felt relief, seeing as I really didn't want to have to cut myself again. Getting cut while still really cold is way more painful than the usual cutting under normal circumstances. I learned that from a minor sledding accident as a kid.

The sound of Tamarr caught my attention. I looked to see that Convile had caught hold of Tamarr's leg and threw him to the floor, where the little guy didn't budge again. I would have gone to him if Convile didn't suddenly turn his knife into a long white staff and point it at me, the end of it glowing a sickly green that didn't bode well for me. He shot the light at Vince and me, and I knew there was no way to escape it.

However, just as it was about to hit us, it hit something else instead. I was surprised to find that we were now protected by a transparent magical pink bubble. Convile looked just as surprised as I felt.

That's when we heard a new voice say, "That will be enough."

Everyone stopped to look at the figure now in the shadows of the entrance. I couldn't make out who it was, but he was clearly important if he could bring everything to a halt like that. Vince looked confused as he listened with his strong vampire hearing. "Wheels?"

I didn't understand, not until the person came into the light. I gasped when I saw him.

It was a man in maybe his late twenties, with bright-blue eyes that seemed to glow and long hair that was pine green down the left side and jet-black down the right. He wore robes like the old wizard, except his were black and white, with silver hemming at the ends of his sleeves and around the edge of his hood, which shadowed his upper face. But what surprised me about him was the wheelchair he sat in. It was extravagant, with plush cushions and what looked like gold detailing and wheels, but it was still very much a wheelchair. It might as well have been a small throne on wheels.

The figure spoke in a dark and powerful voice, quickly reminding me of the power in Jack's voice when he would speak. "You have officially crossed the line with me, Convile."

Convile glared at him. "Ashura."

I was surprised. That was Ashura?

Convile growled, "Men, kill him!"

As the soldiers rushed Ashura, the two guys who had shown up with Tamarr not even bothering to stop them, he waved his short ebony staff, suddenly turning all the soldiers in the room to snow, which collapsed into piles on the floor. I was shocked by how easily he did it, without even batting an eye.

Ashura spoke, his voice growing cold and harsh. "I warned you not to touch my family, Convile. I warned you what I would do to you if you ever laid a finger on her." His eyes were vicious as his pupils became slits, like a cat. "And I am a man of my word." He waved his hand, and the two guys immediately grew wings and flew at Convile. I figured at that point that they were actually vampires like Vince.

As Convile shot off magic and sparks from his staff to keep them back, I hurried over to Tamarr. He still hadn't moved since Convile threw him, and I was worried he was really hurt. I carefully lifted him into my arms. "Tamarr, are you okay? Can you hear me?"

Tamarr shifted before opening his eyes. "I'll be fine." He managed a weak smile. "So long as it worked in keeping you safe, it was worth it."

I smiled. "Thanks for that, Tamarr."

He weakly smiled back.

I was sure he was just glad he could do anything to help, even as a helpless cat, since this did start because they were really after him. I could imagine that Tamarr, having once been a vampire like these guys and Vince, was probably a pretty good fighter, and as a part of the Pumpkin Patch, he probably protected people all the time. Now that he was a cat, he couldn't do any of that anymore, and I was sure, especially with the unbalance and the King of Night causing trouble, that he had a hard time not being able to do more.

I got to my feet as I heard Convile cry out. I looked to see him on the ground underneath the purple-haired vampire, who was sitting pretty comfortably on the old wizard's back, while the other vampire held his staff. I figured Convile couldn't do any magic without it, since he didn't even try to get the vampire off him.

Ashura wheeled himself over, looking down at Convile cruelly. "I warned you, didn't I? I warned you not to touch my niece. I might have let you off for attacking my colleague or threatening these kids since you failed so miserably anyways, but *no one* touches my family and gets away with it."

Convile looked a bit nervous now.

Ashura turned to me and Vince, who was already back on his feet. "Are you all right?"

I looked over at Vince. "I am, but Vince—"

He waved me off. "Don't worry, I'm fine. As I said, it wasn't anything serious since the knife was short." He called that thing short?

Ashura looked at Tamarr in my arms. "And you? I doubt Jack would be forgiving if anything happened to you."

Tamarr smiled, looking tired. "Yeah, I'm all good. This body is way weaker than my old one, but

I'm still a vampire on the inside. I can still take a beating."

Ashura sighed. "Good." He turned his wheelchair around and started out. "Follow me."

I grabbed Vince's hand and followed Ashura out.

He spoke just as he reached the door. "You two know the rules." The two vampires' grins grew as Convile went pale. Ashura wheeled himself out as he said, "He's all yours."

The vampires snickered and looked down at the pale old wizard. I didn't dare look back as I heard Convile start screaming in agony and the sound of tearing and evil laughter began.

Tamarr

I sighed as we stepped into the little bakery again. I still couldn't believe how we all almost just died. If I were still a vampire, I could have easily protected Jason and Vince. I had done it plenty of times before. Sadly, that wasn't the case. As much as I hated it, I wasn't that vampire anymore. Chances were, I never would be again. At least I was able to help a little. That would just have to be enough.

We followed Ashura to a table as he waved for us to sit. He pulled up his wheelchair next to the table as he removed his hood, surprising me by revealing a pair of white cat ears peeking up from his hair. Since when did wizards have brownie ears? Then I remembered him mentioning he was related to the old lady, whom I could tell was a brownie herself. I figured one of his parents must have been a brownie, while the other was a witch or wizard, making him technically both. It was rather rare to meet someone who was a hybrid of two different night creatures, but it was most definitely not impossible.

Vince and Jason sat in the two chairs as Vince sighed. "Well, that was close."

Jason nodded. "No kidding." I noticed him shiver suddenly, clearly still freezing.

I hopped out of his arms and onto the table, already feeling a lot better. "Are you sure you're all right, Jason?"

He nodded softly and said with a weak smile, "Yeah, it's not a big deal. Just cold, that's all." I had a feeling it wasn't just the cold that sent chills down his spine. After all, he had almost been killed too.

I could see Jack's worries materializing before me. The poor guy was just a kid, yet here he was, walking straight toward an already dangerous fate and taking any pains necessary to get there. It was a sad and painful thought. He really didn't deserve this. My ears drooped at the thought of it.

Ashura rubbed my head warmly, clearly understanding my thoughts. "Don't worry, Tamarr. I can tell he's strong. That just might save him in the end." I looked at him and saw the sincerity in his powerful eyes. He gave me a dark smile. "I have a good feeling this time may be much different. Much, much different." I noticed that faraway look in his eyes, just like Jack would get when he'd look in his magic mirror.

Then the old woman from before walked over, looking relieved. "Oh, thank goodness you're all back safely. I was so worried when Convile had his men drag you away."

Ashura smiled at her. "Yes, everyone seems to be all right." His smile wavered for a moment. "How about you, Rebecca? Are you sure you're all right?"

THE DARK EXISTENCE

The woman gave a sweet old smile to reassure him. "Oh, Ashura, you know if I were harmed in any way, I would have told you. I'm just fine. These boys didn't let them hurt me. I'm very grateful to them for their help."

Jason smiled kindly at her. "I'm glad you didn't get hurt because of us."

I sighed. "More like because of me. They only showed up because I was with you. If I hadn't come, they probably never would have bothered you two."

Jason looked at me. "I doubt it. Convile mentioned that he saw us coming through the Grim Reaper's portal, so I think he would have been curious about us anyways."

I knew he was just trying to make me feel better. He really was a good kid.

Rebecca said, "Well, at least now they've found you, Ashura. I would have brought them over, if not for Convile interferring."

Ashura nodded. "Yes, I know. Jack told me they were coming. He would like me to help them with their interesting little quest."

Rebecca giggled. "Sweet Uncle Ashura. There is no soul more loyal and dependable. Your friendship with a prince you don't serve is truly inspiring. That's good friendship. For that, I think a lovely chocolate cake would do nicely right now."

She hurried off to get the cake, which made me chuckle. "Nice old lady."

Jason spoke up. "Okay, I just have to know. Is she really your niece?"

Ashura smirked. "Yes, she is. My great-niece actually."

We all blinked at him in shock.

He smiled as he explained, "What can I say? Wizards age much differently from everyone else. I also discovered the secrets of the fountain of youth, so I look far younger than I actually am."

We gaped at him.

He laughed. "So, yes, Rebecca is my great-niece. She was my youngest sister's second daughter's first child." We still couldn't believe it.

Then Jason spoke again. "And she mentioned that you don't serve under Jack. It's because you don't live in the Night Kingdom, right?"

Ashura nodded softly. "That's right. Jack and I have been dear friends for quite some time. In fact, ever since shortly after Jack was first created, I believe."

Jason was a bit surprised. "Created? What do you mean by that?"

I smiled. "Guess you've never heard of a bexcel, huh?"

Jason shook his head. No surprise, since even many night creatures didn't know what that was.

Ashura explained, "A bexcel is a special kind of night creature that is created of two elements, one for the physical form and the other for the essence of life. It is exceptionally difficult to do, so only the most powerful of night creatures try to create them. And even then, they still run the risk of failure. After all, it's a very intricate process to find two elements that can be formed together to create a stable life."

Jason looked pretty fascinated as Ashura continued. "In Jack's case, he was created from a pumpkin and shadows. The pumpkin, which is actually his head, was given life with the magical essence of shadows. He is really just those two things woven together with powerful yet careful magic to create the bexcel we all know today."

He smirked. "To think that was thirty-eight years ago. I still remember when I heard that the King of Night planned to create a bexcel with such simple elements. I honestly didn't think it would succeed, yet I was pleasantly surprised when I met Jack for the first time. He was indeed everything the king had hoped he would be."

I scoffed. "Until he screwed up and turned Prince Jack into his enemy."

Ashura nodded softly.

That's when Rebecca walked back over. I was surprised when she had a pumpkin on a tray rather than a cake. She looked as confused as we did.

Ashura seemed familiar with this, however. "Um, Rebecca, that's not a cake. That's a pumpkin."

She set it on the table. "Oh, I know, but I don't think the pumpkin knows that."

Just then, jack-o'-lantern eyes opened up on the pumpkin, and little flames danced inside them. I smiled. "Prince Jack!"

Prince Jack's face on the pumpkin slid in my direction as a smile carved itself into the pumpkin.

"I see you are all well." His voice sounded like an echo in the hollowed pumpkin. I was familiar with it, since it was his way of communicating around the Hallows Realm, especially out north.

I glanced at Jason, and he looked amazed. "So that's where the jack-o'-lantern comes in. I knew there had to be a tie in there somewhere."

Jack smiled. "Yes, this is my form of communication. I heard something happened and wanted to make sure everything was all right. Ashura wasn't home when I checked in, so I decided to check in his niece's shop to see if she knew anything." I was still trying to wrap my head around that.

Speaking of Rebecca, she then walked over with the cake. "I found it."

Ashura smiled as she cut a slice for him. "Thank you, Rebecca."

Rebecca looked at Jack. "Would your pumpkin friend like some?"

Jack chuckled and said, "No, thank you, Rebecca. I must be going." He looked over at us. "I just wanted to make sure you three made it safely."

I smiled as Rebecca happily gave me, Jason, and Vince slices of cake. "No need to worry, Prince Jack. We're all peachy." There was no way I was going to tell him about the trouble we had found ourselves in. He had enough on his plate as it was. The fact that no one called me out on my little white lie told me they felt the same way.

He managed a smile. "I'm glad to hear that. I wish you all luck." He looked over at Jason with a sad smile. "Do remember to be careful."

Jason nodded, and it was an ordinary pumpkin once again.

I sighed and looked at Ashura. "Well, I guess you should start telling us where to find the Sorcerer's Crown then."

Ashura sighed and was about to speak, but then his vampires came in. They both had big grins on their faces as they stood at attention. He turned to them as he took a bite of his cake. "You certainly took your time."

They held back their excitement. "Sorry, boss."

Ashura smirked as he used his magic to cut a couple of slices of cake for them. "He's still alive, right? That's the rule."

They nodded as they accepted the floating plates of cake.

The lead one grinned widely. "Barely, but alive. I don't think he'll be bothering anyone for a long while. He'll need that time just to recover."

Ashura chuckled darkly. "Good work."

I was starting to see why he was Prince Jack's ally. Anyone would be afraid to be his enemy, including Prince Jack. Thank goodness he was on our side.

Ashura smiled. "These are my assistants. As you can see, even as a powerful wizard, I do need a little help sometimes." I noticed him glance down at his wheelchair before continuing. "The one in the cap is Oz, and his friend is Sid."

They both gave a respectful bow.

The long-haired one, Oz, grinned. "And my, do we love working for the boss."

Sid smirked. "Truly honored. Certainly a lot better than my old job."

Ashura rolled his eyes, clearly used to this conversation. "You two are just saying that because you get to hurt people for me."

Oz shrugged. "Well, there's that, but who could not love working for an amazing guy like you, boss? Sure, we enjoy the fighting, but we also love having an actual roof over our heads and food to eat, and knowing that we actually have protection from those who would tear us apart and succeed."

Sid nodded. "With everything you've done for us, we'd be honored and privileged to serve you till our dying breath, boss."

Any of us could notice how touched Ashura was, even as he tried to hide it behind a calm, cool front. "Knock that off, you two. You already have the jobs, so there is no need for all this kissing up. Brownnosing isn't a good look for either of you, and I won't have that for assistants of mine."

Sid and Oz only smiled, clearly very familiar with their boss. I couldn't help but smile too. There was no missing how close these three really were.

Ashura then turned his attention to Jason. "Now for why we're all here. The Sorcerer's Crown can be found in the mountains. It's hidden in Caltia Cave. I created the cave with my own magic and sealed it with the pumpkin ring. Tamarr could unseal the cave for you, but from that point, you're on your own."

I was surprised. "What do you mean?"

He sighed. "Jason must go alone to get the crown. That is his test."

I felt worried. "But would he be able to do it? I mean, he's mortal, so how would he manage all alone? No doubt there are traps."

He steepled his fingers. "I'm afraid that's the risk he'll have to take. Trust me, the cave was designed for mortals, so he has as much chance of success as any mortal who has tried before."

Vince was just as concerned about this as I was. "He's already risking his life to use the stupid crown in the first place! Why put him through more than that?"

Jason spoke. "It's okay, guys."

We looked at him.

He smirked. "If I'm gonna save the world, I should do it in style, right? What hero saves the world the easy way? If I gotta pass a test, I'll do it with flying colors. Jack said he'd help me use the crown right. If this is how he'll help me do that, then I'll do it the best I can. I promised him I wouldn't let him down."

I couldn't help but admire the kid.

Ashura clearly felt the same way. "You're very brave. I admire that. I do wish you the best of luck." He turned to his vampires and said, "You two can take them to Caltia Cave."

They gave a nod. "Yes, sir."

Then Oz cleared his throat. "Uh, shouldn't Jason at least get something warm to wear first? He must be freezing to death by now."

I felt a little silly. We had once again forgotten that we were in the frozen North. Jason would need something decent to wear if he was going into those icy caves alone.

Ashura nodded. "Good point. See if you two can find some more decent attire for him first."

They gave a nod and headed out.

Ashura turned to us. "Then you may begin."

Jamal

I walked into the dark room, where Sethra was looking into a crystal ball. I still couldn't believe what my one werewolf had reported to me. He had seen Vince alive, and even more shocking was that the mortal, Jason, was alive and helping him. I had asked if he was sure, and he said he was actually with them in the Hallows Realm.

I walked over to my dear Sethra. Despite the fact I did not make a sound as I walked in, she sensed my presence and spoke. "Something wrong, my darling?"

I sighed. "One of my werewolves just reported to me. Vince is alive."

She spun around. "Vince? Impossible! I made sure he would die! How could he possibly be alive?"

I shook my head, letting my long sleek ponytail move with my head. "I don't know. All I know is, he's alive and in the Hallows Realm."

Her eyes flashed angrily as she turned back to her crystal ball.

I was about to tell her about Jason, but she spoke first. With a sigh, she said, "I suppose I'll just have to kill him again. This time, the right way."

I couldn't understand. "What for? Why kill him again? I still don't understand why that was ever necessary in the first place. It's not like he'd go warn the king of what we were doing."

She chuckled softly. "You have a soft spot for the vampire now, my darling?"

I scoffed. She knew I couldn't stand vampires. "Of course not. What I care about is that you're killing a fellow night creature. Vampires I could care very little for, but the idea of killing them is another thing entirely. They are night creatures, just like us. Why should we kill them? Why kill him? Just because he asks questions? Vampires may be a pain, but they're not stupid. They can tell a lie better than any other night creature. Vince knew we were keeping secrets from him, and he wanted to know why. I don't blame him for that. I'd have done the same thing."

I was silent for a moment before I sighed. "In fact, that's what I'm doing right now. What is the real reason you wish to kill him? Because you don't like him? That's the only reason there is. He's done nothing wrong, nothing to hurt our plans, nothing to stop us. Why bother to kill him again, or even at all?"

Sethra was quiet, but soon she spoke. "You don't trust me?"

I felt a sting of guilt. "Of course, I do. I just don't understand." I looked away as I said, "And I'm concerned. What if his fears about this are right and we fail? What if we do more damage to the realm than the King of Night has already done? To take the crown from him by force? Wouldn't that destroy the balance? The king is supposed to give it up, not be forced through war. No one has ever done it before, so how do we even know if it's possible?"

She didn't look at me.

I felt guilty to admit how little I trusted her plans, but I knew I had to ask sooner or later. Vince's words refused to leave my mind. He used to tell me I was being foolish to just follow along with whatever Sethra said without looking at the end results myself.

I sighed. "When we started, you said we would gather up as many night creatures as we could to stand up against the King of Night, to show him we didn't want him to be king anymore. Then you changed things and decided we had to fight. We had to force him to give up his crown. I went through with it. Then you said we needed more, or we'd risk losing. You said we needed to use that forbidden spell to gain a perfect army. I managed to accept the first change in the plans, but this seems a bit much. That spell is forbidden for a reason. What if it does something we don't suspect? What if it destroys night creatures to be replaced by the mortals we change? To use such a powerful spell, there would have to be some way of balancing it, wouldn't there?"

I was finding that my questions made more sense than I had at first realized. When I looked at it all, I found myself completely against this plan now. Maybe that vampire was on to something after all. Perhaps I was being foolish to follow Sethra, just as he had said. Maybe vampires were smarter than I thought. Well, I suppose that was obvious, seeing as he was alive and well when he should have been long dead.

Sethra sighed. "You're asking a lot of questions, Jamal. Just like that vampire." She turned to me, with no feeling in her eyes.

I sighed. "Sethra, I don't think we should continue this. There are too many risks. And for what? More unbalance? What do we really gain by doing things this way?"

She smiled at me. "You know how I feel about being questioned, Jamal."

I felt a chill down my spine. I knew she hated to be questioned. That was probably the biggest reason she had tried to kill Vince. I had a good feeling she didn't care whether he was a vampire or not; he had questioned her, and he had paid the price. Even if he did live, I heard he had still ended up blind.

Sethra shook her head, with a chuckle that made me take a step back from her. "Oh, Jamal, you know I don't appreciate being questioned."

I spoke up, though I felt fear creep in. "Sethra, I'm not questioning you. I'm just concerned—worried even."

She laughed. "I should have known you would fail me too, Jamal. Should have known you were too weak."

I felt my werewolf pride start to replace my fear. "I agreed to this plan because I love you, Sethra. Because I want to see the king stopped. Because I want to help save our world before it's too late. It is not weakness to rethink this plan. It's wise. Too many night creatures will get hurt, including you. I'm just looking out for you, Sethra."

She looked at me with icy eyes. "I don't need you, Jamal. I never did." She pulled out a long, thin metal staff with a star at the top, in a glass orb.

I took a couple of steps back. "Sethra…"

She grinned as the staff started to glow a deathly green. "I can't have you getting in my way, Jamal. Love doesn't replace the King of Night's crown. I will be queen."

I felt horror at her statement. "Vince was right. You are after the crown."

She grinned evilly as I found myself cornered, and her staff's glow grew brighter. "You've served your purpose."

The glow grew brighter, and I knew with horror what it meant.

I remembered all that my werewolf had told me—how Vince and Jason were going for the Sorcerer's Crown to stop Sethra. I glared at her. "You won't get away with this, Sethra. Even if I die, there are others who are out there to stop you." I smiled darkly at her. "You will fall, and if you do manage to live when your plan fails, I'll haunt you the rest of your miserable life. That is a promise."

The upper half of Sethra's face was shadowed by the bright-green glow of her staff, making her glowing red eyes stand out with her evil grin. "Goodbye, 'my love.'"

The green light grew immensely bright. Then everything went black.

SETHRA

My staff stopped glowing as I looked down at the lifeless body of Jamal. His long sleek hair had fallen from its band, and his dark skin was soft and perfect like an angel's. I had always loved his perfect beauty. His werewolf form was hideous, and his wolf form was simple. It was a shame he had to go. Sad, pathetic fool.

This was that miserable vampire's fault. He got into the pup's head. But it didn't matter anymore. It was time for another change of plans.

I left the room and walked down the hall of my castle. My latest partner, Flynn, was waiting outside the room, so he walked with me. I had chosen him as my replacement for Vince—someone who could have a strong effect on people to gain their trust. Vince used to do that since he was a vampire and had a charm and power of persuasion that won over just about anyone, especially the vampires who were loyal to him.

Flynn was a handsome young man—not as handsome as Jamal was, of course, but he was a very powerful wizard. His short blue hair had long bangs, and his eyes were bicolored. The left one was midnight blue, while the right one was a glowing gold, without a pupil. It was his magic eye. Unlike me and other wielders of magic, he didn't need a staff or wand to do powerful magic. Though he had to be a couple of years younger than me, that didn't change his potential for power with that magic eye.

His long black-and-silver robes brushed against the floor as he walked by my side. "Where is Jamal?"

I spoke without any remorse or sorrow. "He's dead."

Flynn looked surprised, then annoyed. "Are you insane? You killed him? Do you have any idea what you've just done?"

I sighed. "Yes, I know."

He rolled his eyes, clearly aggravated with me. "Well, obviously you don't, because he's dead! With him dead, the werewolves will revolt! The plan is ruined! We need vampires, werewolves, and witches or wizards for the spell to work! We're lucky I managed to persuade enough vampires to join us. Luckily, no one knows that the first vampire is dead yet."

I groaned. "He's not dead."

Flynn stopped. "Excuse me?"

I stopped and turned back to him, my long blue dress sweeping the floor. "He's not dead. Somehow he survived my spell."

Flynn's eyes flashed with irritation. "Are you kidding me? We've now got a dead werewolf prince in there, and the vampire who doesn't agree with our plans and who could turn every vampire in the realm against us is *alive*?"

I sighed. "So it seems."

He pinched the bridge of his nose with one hand and put his other hand to his hip. "This plan is a complete and utter failure."

I straightened up. "The plan will work. We've come too far to fail now!"

He put his other hand to his other hip. "Oh, right, and just what do you plan to tell Jamal's werewolves? We killed their leader, but they should still help us? Or maybe you could try your chances on saying the King of Night killed him for turning traitor? The werewolves may still not stay. They barely trust you as it is."

I waved him off. "I'll take care of the werewolves. I'll just tell them Jamal is taking care of unfinished business for me. They'll believe it. He was obsessed with me."

Flynn smirked. "Oh, yeah, he's just gonna spend the next few days taking care of unfinished business without any word to his werewolves? And he still won't return to help with the plan? Yeah, that should work."

I glared at him. "Watch it, boy. I could—"

He smirked. With a roll of his eyes, he cut me off. "You could what? Kill me too? Oh, yeah, because anyone is going to bother sticking with you once I go missing too. You think your plans are in trouble now? Wait until they find out just what you really are!"

I glared at him, then turned away. He was right. I couldn't do this alone, as much as I preferred to. I needed him. I sighed and started walking down the hall. "Fine. Then we'll just have to make a change of plans."

Flynn caught up with me and gave me a curious yet very cautious look. "And what change would that be?"

I smiled darkly without looking at him. "We can't wait until Hallows' Eve night. By then, the werewolves will know something's up. We won't give them a chance to think about it."

He was very curious now. "What will you do?"

I grinned at him. "We're not waiting anymore. We're doing this *tonight*."

Tamarr

I stood on Jason's shoulder as he and the other vampires climbed up the mountain. After climbing so high we couldn't see the town below anymore through all the snow and wind, before us stood a large flat wall of the mountain. Vince had been on Sid's back as he easily climbed with incredible strength, even for a vampire. Now he stood beside us, listening to the wind hitting the flat wall before us.

He smirked. "Wow, talk about an obvious place to 'hide' a cave. Lucky it's up this high, where no one below can see it, or everyone would easily guess the crown is hidden here."

Oz turned to me and said, "Okay, the boss said your pumpkin ring can open the cave."

I raised my tail up high, revealing my pumpkin ring as it began to glow, trying to connect its power to the wall the way it normally would connect to the pumpkin ring of a comrade.

It didn't take long before the wall started to groan and rumble as my ring's glow turned to gold. We stood back as a large crack ran up the center of the wall and slowly opened before us. I was amazed. I had never seen someone create something so simple yet so impressive. It only showed how powerful a wizard Ashura was. Soon enough, the rumbling stopped, and the cave sat open to us.

Jason sighed. "I guess I'd better go in." He let me hop onto Oz's shoulder, who scratched me behind my ears, which I loved so much. Jason looked over at us. "Wish me luck." I could tell he was getting nervous.

I smiled, trying to keep his spirits up. "You'll do fine."

Vince smiled. "Yeah. You're the bravest kid I've ever met. If anyone can do it, it's you."

Jason looked touched by our encouragement. Oz and Sid gave him thumbs-up and encouraging grins.

He smirked. "Thanks, guys." He turned to the cave and took a deep breath. "Here goes nothing."

With that, he walked in. We watched him go.

When he was so far in, the cave started to close. Jason looked back, a little more worried. I smiled and called out to him as the rumbling cave started to shut itself. "We'll be waiting right here for you when you get back. We promise."

Then the cave was gone, and a solid flat wall stood before us. It was as if the cave, and Jason, had never been there at all.

I sighed. "Good luck, Jason."

JASON

I only stared at the blank wall that separated me from the others. I noticed it wasn't a pitch-black cave. The walls had strange glowing teal lines, like veins, running down the tunnel I was in. I sighed. "I guess there's no going back now."

I started down the tunnel, following the beautiful veins of light. I wondered what it was, but I remembered how Ashura said he had made the cave himself. I figured it was just his own handiwork. I thought it was pretty neat and creative. I thought to myself as I walked. *I wonder if I'll ever see any of them again.*

I remembered what Tamarr said just before the cave closed. They'd be waiting right outside for me when I come out. I couldn't help but smile. He had sounded so sure when he said it that I couldn't find it in myself not to believe him. I would be fine. I just had to do my best. They, my whole world, this world, and Jack were all depending on me.

I thought about Jack again. I couldn't shake that feeling that he reminded me of someone I once knew, but no matter how hard I tried, I couldn't remember. Then I thought of what I saw in the mirror in his throne room. I was just a kid in my reflection. Why? Was there a tie to what I couldn't remember? I just wished I could have seen Jack's reflection clearer.

Then I heard something ahead of me down the tunnel. I looked to see a turn up ahead. I could tell something was around that corner. I stepped up to the edge of the tunnel, leaning against the wall. I peeked around the corner to see something horrifying.

There was a giant spider, asleep before large stone doors. I felt sweat bead on my forehead, even though the cave was freezing. There were frozen webs made entirely of ice in every corner of the tunnel with the giant spider. The spider was even white and blue, like ice.

I pulled back and leaned against the wall with a deep sigh. What was I doing? What was I thinking? I couldn't do this. It was insane to have ever thought I could. I was literally trapped in a nightmare. I couldn't do it. I was going to die there alone.

"Don't be afraid, Jason."

I heard the voice at the back of my mind. The voice was familiar, but I couldn't put a name to it. It was so far and deep in the back of my mind, almost like it was locked back there. It gave me that same feeling of familiarity as Jack, like I knew something I just couldn't remember.

I sat down with my back against the wall and let the voice come back to me. It was hard to do since it was so far back in my mind. I tried looking at the spider and thinking about how terrified I was.

THE SILVER SPARROW

Then the voice surfaced again. *"Don't be afraid, Jason. I'm right here."*

I tried to dwell on it as it tried to submerge in my lost memories again. If I could just remember that voice, maybe I could remember everything else. I couldn't stand not remembering anymore.

Then I remembered when I was ten and how I was hit by a truck and lost my memories of that entire year. I never did get those memories back. I even constantly forget it ever happened, especially since my parents refused to ever talk about it afterward. I started to wonder if these memories weren't from that year. I tried to resurface more by thinking about when I first laid eyes on Jack and how familiar he felt. I felt something, but I needed more.

I thought about when I looked in the mirror. I remembered how I had looked like just a kid—a ten-year-old kid. The feeling got stronger. It felt like I was about to break something blocking my memories.

Then I thought about the voice.

"Don't be afraid. Don't be afraid, Jason."

Suddenly, the block snapped, and I was hit with memories I never knew I had. The sudden flood of memories was so overwhelming that I finally collapsed. As I lay there on the stone floor, I could only manage to make out one last thought.

I was right.

JASON

I woke up one morning to the sound of a truck outside. I sat up in my race car-shaped bed, wondering what it could be. I quickly jumped out of bed and hurried to the window. I smiled with glee when I spotted what was out there. There was a moving truck at the house across the street. Someone was moving into my neighborhood, meaning maybe finally someone I could make friends with.

I hurried out of my bedroom and down the hall. I stopped at my parents' room and turned the doorknob, throwing open the door and hurrying inside. My mom and dad were asleep in bed together as I climbed up and crawled to where their heads were sound asleep.

I tapped my dad. "Dad, wake up. We have new neighbors."

My dad, who looked like an adult version of me, opened his eyes and looked at me. "What is it, Jason?"

I smiled in my excitement. "There's new people moving in across the street."

My mom woke up with a beautiful smile, her long brown hair pulled back into a braid, as it always was overnight. "Hey there, honey."

I smiled at her. "Mom, we have new neighbors across the street!"

She smiled pleasantly. "That sounds nice, sweetie. We should go visit later."

I smiled excitedly and hurried off the bed. I ran off to my room, where I changed and put on my favorite baseball cap. I had gotten it from a baseball game I attended with my dad earlier that year.

I hurried downstairs and found my mom making a bowl of cereal for me. I hopped onto the chair as she set it in front of me, and I said, "Thanks, Mom!"

My dad came down and turned on the coffee maker. My baby brother laughed as my dad yawned. He always thought Dad looked funny when he yawned. Dad smiled and got out a mug.

My mom smiled as our usual morning routine continued, and she asked, "Should we take a gift basket over to our new neighbors, Jason?"

I nodded. "Yeah!"

I finished my cereal and helped my mom make the gift basket. It was full of cookies and other treats, one of the bonuses of having a mom who owned her own bakery. I hurried outside while my mom got baby David. Once I was out there, I saw people on the other side of the street. There was a man, a woman, and a boy several years older than I was, looking up at their new house with their backs to me.

Suddenly, there was a gust of wind that blew my cap right off my head. "My cap!"

I hurried after it as it flew across the street, up in the air where I couldn't reach it. That's when the boy hopped up and caught it. I smiled and ran over. He smiled as he turned to me and held it out. "Here you go, kid."

I took my cap gratefully. "Thanks!"

I looked up at the boy. He had black hair and yellow-orange eyes that seemed darker orange around the edges. He smiled at me with a smile much like my mom's, pleasant and caring. "So you're one of my new neighbors?"

I nodded. "Uh-huh! I'm Jason Conner!"

He looked pleased. "Jason Conner. Nice to meet you, Jason. I'm Oden Lantern. Just got here today."

I nodded again. "I know! I saw your big moving truck drive here!"

He chuckled. "You did? Wow, you must be super observant."

I was confused. "Obzerbant?"

He laughed kindly. "Observant. It means you pay extra close attention to things."

I smiled proudly. "Yeah! I'm very observant!"

He laughed, amused by my childish nature. For a ten-year-old, I was not quite as mature as the other kids on my street. It was part of why I couldn't really make any friends back then.

Then my mom walked over, with David clinging to her skirt and the gift basket in one hand. "Hello there."

Oden smiled kindly at her. "Hi, you must be Mrs. Conner."

She smiled back, shaking his hand. "I am. I'm Laura Conner."

Oden went down in front of David. "And who might you be?"

David hid behind my mom's legs, with his thumb in his mouth.

My mom watched with that smile I loved so much. "This is David, and I see you've met my son Jason."

Oden stood up and smiled. "Yeah, he's a cool kid."

I smiled up at my mom. "He saved my favorite baseball cap!"

She giggled as she patted my head. "He did? That was very nice of him. Did you say thank you?"

I nodded. "Yes, ma'am."

Oden motioned to the house. "Why don't you come in? We've got most of the furniture moved in, and my parents would love to meet you all."

We followed him into the house. It was really big. The living room was already set up, and the movers were getting stuff into the kitchen in the next room. We met Oden's mom and an uncle who was just helping them move in, neither very talkative. Oden did most of the talking, and they just smiled. They smiled a lot.

I remembered my mom giving the family their gift basket and Oden talking about how they had moved into the neighborhood for his dad's job. I remembered him saying, "My dad messed something up at his job, so we had to come here to fix it. He should be joining us in a few months' time."

My mom was curious. "What did he mess up?"

Oden was hesitant, but he smiled as he replied, "He works for… the police. He lost one of the men he was supposed to *deal* with. We moved here to see if we could find him."

My mom was surprised. "Oh dear, should we be worried?"

He smiled. "Not at all. He won't hurt anyone. He's harmless right now, wherever he is. We're just concerned about what he might do when he's older." He caught himself. "I just mean what he might do in the future." I noticed he looked a little worried about something, but I was too young to understand.

*****

As the months went by, I became close friends with Oden. He was like a big brother to me. I did everything with him, from playing catch, to going to the park, to even sleeping over.

One day, I was at the pool with him and my family. It was a hot summer day. I stood away from the pool, where Oden had pulled off his T-shirt, attracting plenty of attention from the nearby girls.

He smiled at me in my trunks. "Aren't you going in the pool, Jason?"

I shook my head.

THE SILVER SPARROW

He looked at me curiously. "Why not? Can't you swim?"

I shook my head again.

He smiled and went down beside me. "You want me to teach you?"

I still only shook my head.

He gave it some thought. "Then would you like to go in the kiddie pool?"

I shook my head once more.

He smiled patiently, trying to understand what was wrong. "Why not?"

I stared at my feet. "Because I'm too big. Only up to five years old can go in."

Oden tilted his head slightly, still taking his time to figure out what was going on with me. "You mean you never go in the pool when you come here?"

I was quiet, but then I sighed. "I used to go in the big pool, but… I sank last year. My stomach started to hurt really bad, and I couldn't swim." I shivered, remembering the awful experience.

He seemed a bit confused at first, then he seemed to remember something. "Oh, so you had… stomach cramps, is it? You probably ate right before you went swimming, right?"

I nodded. "I don't wanna go in the big pool. I don't want to sink again."

He looked thoughtful and even a bit sympathetic. "So you can swim, but you're afraid?"

I nodded sadly.

He gave it some thought before giving me a confident smile. "Then we need to conquer that fear."

THE DARK EXISTENCE

I felt afraid and shook my head. "No, I don't wanna!"

He smiled, a look that always seemed to help me feel better. "Don't you trust me? I promise I can help you beat your fear."

I felt unsure. Of course, I trusted him, more than anyone, but…

He took my hand. "You can trust me. I won't let you get hurt. I promise."

I let him lead me to the pool. My heart started racing as he climbed in, leaving me at the side.

He treaded water there with a smile. "See, it's safe. I'm not sinking. Now you come in. I'll be right here."

I felt really nervous and didn't budge.

A man waiting to get in groaned from behind me. "Move it, kid."

Oden gave him a look that easily shut him up.

I looked at the water and said, "I can't."

Oden seemed to consider something, before making up his mind and speaking with a kind smile. "Don't be afraid." The words seemed to echo in my mind. "*Don't be afraid, Jason.*"

I looked at him.

He smiled kindly. "Don't be afraid, Jason. I'm right here."

I felt the fear wash away slowly. A wave of courage seemed to come over me for the very first time. I climbed down into the water and started treading beside Oden.

He smiled happily. "You see? You did it!"

I smiled back. "Yeah, I did."

He stayed next to me as the man from earlier climbed in behind us. "If you want, you can stay close to me, just in case you get any tummy troubles again. Okay?"

I nodded, feeling pretty proud of myself. "Okay. Thanks, Oden."

*****

Another day, I remembered there was a birthday party at the house of a kid from my school. I asked Oden, who was babysitting David and me that night, to take me, and he said yes. That night, at the party, everything was going great; and everyone was having fun until something very strange happened.

Not being careful as I plugged the radio into an outlet under a table, I accidentally touched the prong and got a small zap. Suddenly, out of nowhere, all the balloons started to pop, the lights flickered on and off, and soda bottles exploded. All the little kids started screaming and running, even after it all stopped.

Oden was down beside me in an instant. "Are you okay, Jason?"

I was sucking my finger, not used to getting an electric shock. I showed it to him. "I'm fine. I just hurt my finger."

He looked surprised, then worried. He looked around the room at all the chaos.

THE DARK EXISTENCE

Finally, he helped me up and said, "Let's get you home, okay? Where's David?"

I pointed to one of the moms at the party who was holding David. David was crying from the earlier noise, like all the other little kids. Oden got him and took my hand, and we left for home.

I looked up at Oden, who looked really upset about something as we walked home. I finally spoke up. "Are you mad at me, Oden?"

He looked at me, a bit surprised by my question, as we walked down the empty street. "No, of course not. I'm just…" He looked sad. "I was… worried you got hurt." He looked ahead, still sad.

Then David spoke up, holding out his little finger. "Booboo."

Oden looked. "Oh, you hurt your finger too, David? Probably during the… event."

David nodded and laid his head on Oden's shoulder.

Oden smiled softly. "We'll take you home and get a bandage for it, okay?"

David nodded without lifting his head.

I spoke up. "Me too."

Oden smiled sadly. "Yeah, you too, Jason."

I didn't understand why he was sad, but I remembered that when my mom was sad, she didn't like to talk about it. So I just let him take us home.

The next day, Oden seemed sad all day. I tried everything, but he just didn't seem to get out of that mood. It soon got even stranger.

That afternoon, Oden's cell phone rang. He answered it as he watched TV, with me sitting next to him. "Lantern speaking."

He looked surprised. "Wait, slow down. What happened?" He went pale as he listened to the person on the other side.

He scared me by suddenly jumping to his feet. "What?" He listened a moment, his expression a bit panicked. "But that's impossible, isn't it? He can't do that! He wouldn't do that! Why would…?" He listened and looked furious. "And you're sure he… And they…?"

I watched him from the couch, wondering what was wrong.

He sighed, both worried and angry. "All right. All right, just keep things in order till then."

Then he hung up and sighed miserably. He said softly to himself, "What have you done?"

He must have remembered me at that moment because he turned to me with kind eyes. I was holding a pillow tightly. He smiled, trying to comfort me. "I'm sorry. I didn't mean to scare you, Jason."

I looked up at him and spoke quietly. "Did that person make you mad, Oden?"

He sat beside me. "No. That was a friend of mine from my hometown, who was telling me about someone else who made me mad."

I looked at the pillow on my lap. "Did I make you sad, Oden?"

He looked a bit confused. "Of course not. Why would you ask that?"

THE DARK EXISTENCE

I felt sad as I said, "You were sad all day. Ever since last night."

He looked as kind and patient as ever as he answered, "You didn't make me sad, Jason. It was something else entirely."

I looked at him again. "Were you sad you went to the party with me?"

He shook his head softly, sitting closer to me. "No. I was glad I went with you. The only thing about that party that made me sad was that you and David got hurt. I should have watched you both closer."

I tried to cheer him up. "But I'm okay now, so you don't have to be sad." I showed him my finger, wanting him to see I was all better.

He chuckled softly, a soft look of compassion in his eyes. "I see. That's good. But as I said, I was sad about something else. Okay?"

I smiled in relief. "Okay."

*****

The next morning, I heard noise outside. I looked out my window and gasped. There was a moving truck outside of Oden's house. I hurried out of bed, got changed, and raced downstairs. My mom was already up and cooking, my dad had already gone to work, and David was in his high chair. I ignored my mom as she asked where I was going.

THE SILVER SPARROW

I ran outside to Oden's house. He was standing outside, just like he had been the day he first arrived. I ran over. "Oden!"

He looked at me, looking sad again.

I rushed over and hugged him. "Please don't move away!"

Oden looked down at me sadly as he said, "I'm sorry, Jason, but I have to go."

I had tears in my eyes. "Why?"

He looked deeply upset and sad. "Well, I have friends who really need me right now. Something really bad happened, and I have to go help fix it."

Tears rolled down my face as I continued to plead with him. "But I don't want you to go. I want you to stay!"

His eyes were glassy as he tried not to show how hurt he was inside. "I'm sorry, Jason."

I held him close, and he hugged me back tightly.

Then I heard Mrs. Lantern call from the car. "Time to go, Oden." She was still smiling that big smile.

I let go of Oden and wiped my eyes.

Oden went down in front of me. "Jason." I looked at him as he smiled kindly. "I'm so glad I met you."

I sniffled miserably. "I'll never forget you."

He looked pained before speaking again. "Actually, I think it's best you don't remember. It's better neither of us does."

I didn't understand.

THE DARK EXISTENCE

He smiled as he took my cheek in one hand. "Just promise me you'll be good. Okay? No matter what, you'll be the same wonderful kid you are now. You have a big heart and a good head on your shoulders. Don't ever lose that, okay?"

I nodded. "I promise."

With that, he stood up. "You should go home now."

I nodded and ran off for home. I thought I heard Oden say weird words, but just when I looked back, suddenly there was a truck headed for me.

I heard my mom scream my name, but just as it came at me—

JASON

I gasped and woke up. I was on the floor, panting and cold. I sat up and saw the cave around me. I was in Caltia Cave. I glanced around the corner, and there lay the giant spider, still fast asleep. I exhaled deeply and leaned back, letting my head lie back against the cold stone wall. I wasn't the ten-year-old kid anymore. I was seventeen now, and I was in the Hallows Realm, trying to find the Sorcerer's Crown so I could stop the evil witch Sethra.

I groaned and let the memories I just saw run through my mind. Oden. Oden Lantern. I couldn't believe it. I had seen Jack before after all. Prince Jack-O'-Lantern was actually Jack-*Oden*-Lantern. I started to feel annoyed. So Jack did know me the whole time, and he didn't tell me.

Or did he? Did he know me? He said it was better neither of us remembered. What if he erased his own memory too? Could he have had something to do with me getting hit by a truck? Had that been his way of taking away my memory?

I only sighed. It didn't matter. I was still in Caltia Cave, facing the impossible. I was never going to get a chance to ask him now. I was never going to see him again at all.

Then I thought of when we were at the pool, how he taught me to just face my fear. Though that was just a pool. This was a giant spider that would eat me, and who knew what else after that. Don't get me started on the freaking crown of insanity I would have to wear and stop an evil witch with.

This really was insane. What was I thinking? I couldn't do this. This wasn't like the pool at all. And this time, he wasn't right here with me. No one was here this time.

Yet for some reason, I stood up and took a deep breath. I was going to do it. That wave of confidence washed over me again. If I didn't do this, a lot of good people, including my little brother and Jack and Vince, were going to die. I had to at least try, right?

I looked around the corner at the spider. I gulped before I began tiptoeing toward the doors. I was silent as I stepped over icicle webs and spider legs. I imagined that the spider was the water from the pool and the doors were Oden waiting for me.

"Don't be afraid, Jason."

Even all these years later, those words stuck to my mind in a way nothing else ever had, and it gave me a sense of courage nothing else ever could.

I stepped over the last spider leg and reached the doors. I felt so much relief. I had made it.

I pushed open one of the doors, only for it to groan under its own weight. I felt my heart stop at the sound. I quickly noticed the movement behind me. I didn't wait to see what it was—not that I really needed to.

I hurried through the door and started pushing it shut. Spider legs kept reaching through the closing door at me. With one last grunt of effort, I shut it, snapping a couple of the spider legs off at my feet. I jumped back from them in fright. They just lay there as I stood panting. I tried to slow my heart down by breathing in through my nose and out through my mouth. It was a breathing exercise I learned in PE.

I turned to see down the tunnel I was in. The veins of light in the walls were red now. I walked down the tunnel in silence. I could only hope I wasn't walking into another death trap. Something told me I was.

I stopped at the next turn. I peeked around the corner to see a wide cave with doors at the end. The veins traveled all over the walls and the dome ceiling, bathing the room in red light. I didn't see anything else in the room, though I did notice it was warmer in that cave. I wanted to take off my coat, but I thought against it. I didn't know what I was up against or if I'd be able to grab my coat in a hurry if things got bad, and I'd need my coat for when I got out.

I smiled. *When* I got out. Not if. I was already feeling pretty confident about this. Funny how I seemed to keep getting those surges of courage. I wondered if maybe Oden had done something I didn't know about. I'd have to ask later. I took a deep breath and ran across the cave.

THE DARK EXISTENCE

Suddenly, a geyser of lava burst from the ground ahead of me. I stopped and jumped back to miss being torched. I ran past it, just to stop for another one. I hurried past that one too. Over and over, as I ran for the doors, lava would burst out. I was almost there when I realized that lava was pouring along the ground toward me. I kept running until I reached the doors. I pushed them, though I quickly found that they were extremely heavy. I managed to squeeze myself through and hurried to close them as the lava came my way. Just as the lava reached the doors, I got them closed.

I fell on my butt with a relieved sigh. That was, once again, very close. "Man, Ashura certainly made some crazy tests in here."

I stood up and dusted myself off before I looked around to see that I was in yet another tunnel. This time, the light was yellow. Somehow I felt that I was close. I walked down the tunnel, letting the glow relax me. With every obstacle I passed, I began to feel more confident.

I soon reached large stone doors. No caves, no turns, no giant creatures. I stood before the doors, curious about what was to come next. I took a breath and shoved the heavy doors open.

I walked into the enormous cave on the other side. It reached incredibly high into the air. In the center of the room was a huge pillar of stone that reached almost to the top of the cave. Along the walls were teal veins like the first tunnel, except this time they were going up in a spiral to the very top of the dome ceiling. Some even spiraled up the pillar.

From where I stood, I could see a bright glow at the top of the pillar. I groaned as I eyed the top. "How am I supposed to get up there?"

I looked around to see nothing useful. I walked up to the pillar to see that it was too smooth to climb. I stuffed my hands into my pockets. "Great. I get here, and I can't even get to the top." I looked up at the light again. I wondered if it was the crown glowing up there. I groaned. "There has to be something around here for a mortal to use to reach the top. Ashura would—"

Then the veins around the pillar started turning gold going up, but only a short way, then it stopped. At the same height was the beginning of a staircase of shadows.

I was surprised. "Ashura?"

Nothing happened.

I gave it some thought. "Well, obviously it went up because I said Ashura's name, but what else do I say?"

I grinned confidently as an idea came to mind. "Maybe I have to think of the rest of a sentence." I thought it over a bit. "Ashura... is... awesome?" Nothing. "Ashura... has... fungus?" Still nothing, but I laughed.

I tried again. "Ashura... and... Tamarr... are—"

I was cut off when the gold glow rose higher, making more stairs, and then stopped. I grinned. "So it's names I'm supposed to say, huh?" I went up to the

THE DARK EXISTENCE

top of the steps as I spoke. "Ashura. Tamarr. Vince?" Nothing. I rubbed my chin. "There must be a pattern. What ties Ashura and Tamarr together?"

I smirked. "That's easy. Tin." The glowing rose, along with the stairs. I understood. "It's the names of the Pumpkin Patch. Grim Reaper." It rose again. "Krank." It rose yet again.

It was over halfway up, but then I groaned. "But I don't know anymore. Those are the only ones I've met or heard of so far. Besides Jack." It rose once more. I scratched my head as I tried to think. "I have to know someone else. Anyone else." I noticed I was close to the top. If I had maybe a couple more names, I could reach the edge and pull myself up.

I decided to just use any name I could think of and hope I got lucky. "Rose. Melody. Melora. Berleen. Leanndra. Veil. Fen. Michael. David. Laura. Oden. Ja—"

I almost fell off the stairs as they rose again. Oden. I grinned as I got my balance. "Figures." I looked up at the edge again. "Well, there's no way I'm gonna know any more names."

I took a deep breath and squatted down. I was really hoping I wouldn't fall. I jumped up, reaching for the ledge. I just missed, falling back down and almost falling off the steps. I managed to get my balance back and gave a sigh of relief. I took a deep breath and tried again. I caught the ledge, but not well enough. I landed back on my feet. I prepared myself. "Third time's the charm." I jumped again and grinned when I caught and stayed. I pulled myself up with all my strength.

With one big push, I was up on the platform. I lay on my back and sighed, letting my legs hang over the side. I opened my eyes and gasped. There was an altar standing over me, looking like a miniature version of the pillar I was on at that moment. I stood up and faced it. It was just above my waist in height.

I stood before it and looked at the bright glowing object floating about an inch above it—a gold circlet with a violet diamond-shaped jewel at the center. The Sorcerer's Crown. I could feel the power emanating from it. I smiled, feeling rather accomplished. "I made it."

I hesitantly reached out to touch it, remembering what everyone said about it and what they said it would do to me. That thought made me stop. Was I really ready for this? Could I really be strong enough to handle it? I took a deep breath, remembering why I was here and what I would be protecting, and reached for it again. My finger just touched it when it started glowing incredibly bright, blinding me. As the light engulfed everything, I could feel something tighten around my head.

Suddenly, the light was gone. I felt my head and found that the crown fitted perfectly around it, sitting just beneath my hairline. It didn't hurt at all, but when I tried to take it off, it wouldn't budge. It was almost like it was a part of my head now. I groaned. "Okay, they could have at least told me it's a permanent accessory." I sighed, smiling in spite of it. "But

I got the crown, so now I can leave." I hopped down the stairs and hurried down them.

When I reached the floor, I remembered. Now what? How was I supposed to leave? The one cave was probably leaking with lava, and the other tunnel had a big evil spider waiting for me with its last six legs. I wondered how I was going to get out, when I heard someone far off cry out. I was surprised as I recognized it. "Vince?"

SETHRA

I stood over all the witches, wizards, and werewolves that now served me. There were hundreds in my ballroom, most of them on the floor while several vampires were flying above us. I smiled, standing over them from a balcony. "Greetings, my companions! There has been a change of plans. We will be moving out *tonight*!"

The witches and wizards cheered, but the werewolves looked as concerned as the vampires. One werewolf, a handsome dark-skinned redhead, walked over. "Why? And where is our leader?"

I gave my most pleasant and innocent smile. "He is bravely taking care of some unfinished business for me. He will be joining us later. Right now, he has allowed me to move you all out into battle. We will not wait any longer!"

The werewolves, besides the one who questioned me, joined the cheer. That werewolf was no doubt Ronan, Jamal's childhood friend whom Jamal had told me about. If anyone might figure out Jamal was dead, it would be him. I'd have to *deal* with him later.

THE DARK EXISTENCE

Flynn watched from the sidelines, his hood shadowing his face. I had always found him so enchanting in his dark ways. Maybe if he were older and more powerful, I might have considered him for a new toy to replace Jamal. Sadly, Flynn was not nearly as gullible as Jamal was. His family history also played a dangerous part in my avoiding getting too close.

I raised my staff. "Tonight we invade the mortal realm and fight war with the King of Night to save our realm!"

They all cheered, though some vampires looked unconvinced. Clearly, they could sense something wrong about my plan—and me. They could do as they liked, for I was finally on my way to victory.

Then I remembered what Jamal said. I said to the crowd, "But first, it seems we have a little delay. I need ten werewolves to come with me and help me take care of some business. Flynn will stay and make sure things go smoothly at the invasion point."

Ten werewolves stepped forward.

I smiled, barely hiding my enjoyment. "We have a little exterminating to do."

JASON

I heard it again and knew something was wrong. "Vince?" I hurried to the sound, which was coming from behind one of the walls. I leaned against the wall, listening. I could hear noises somewhere on the other side. I stood back. "Okay, crown, if you're gonna be useful, now's the time."

The jewel on the crown started to glow. I held out my hand toward the wall, feeling that it was the right thing to do, and violet light flew out of it, knocking me back on my butt. The light hit the wall, creating a nicely sized hole. I hurried to my feet and went through it before it could try to close like the cave entrance. I stepped out into the freezing cold and saw that I was way up high on the mountainside.

I looked down the snowy mountainside and saw Vince hanging on to a ledge, trying his hardest not to fall down the cliff. A couple of wolves were growling at him as if threatening him to try to come back up. Clearly, they couldn't reach him. He had probably tripped and fell. I heard other sounds and saw Oz and Sid fighting off a few other wolves, while Tamarr hid in the vest of Sid's clothes, probably afraid of being eaten by all these wolves. I knew I had to help Vince myself.

I felt that wave of courage again and yelled down. "Hang on, Vince!"

Vince gasped upon hearing my voice. "Jason?"

The wolves heard me and ran in my direction. I thought of a way to stop them, and the crown did it for me. The snow around the wolves' feet suddenly sprang up around them and froze, locking their legs in ice. They couldn't move. I hurried past them as they snapped their jaws at me. I stopped at the slippery edge, trying not to fall. "Just hang on, Vince."

Vince smiled, deeply relieved. "You made it out. I figured you would."

I was glad to hear his confidence in me. "Yep, and I've got the crown. Now try to reach out to me."

He did, and I managed to grab his hand before he could fall. I pulled him up and helped him back up past the wolves, which I started to figure were werewolves. Vince had mentioned their wolf forms once before.

We reached the others, who had finished with their werewolves. They smiled at me. "You're alive!"

Tamarr's little head popped out of Sid's clothes with a bright smile. "I knew you would make it."

I couldn't help the warmth I felt upon seeing them so proud of me. "Well, you were right. Now let's go. We have to go tell Ashura and Jack."

ASHURA

I was alone as I sat outside Rebecca's shop under the cloudy, darkening evening sky. I was beginning to worry. They had been gone a while, and I had no way of knowing how the kid was doing.

I held a pumpkin on my lap. I was waiting for when Jack would start worrying and contact me. I knew he would soon. He always had a big heart for others, especially when they were in danger. I also didn't want him frightening Rebecca when he did, so I kept the pumpkin with me.

I stared up at the mountains in the distance. I had figured the others would wait outside the cave for him like good friends. I hoped they were all right.

Then the pumpkin started to speak. "Ashura? Are you there?"

I sighed patiently. "I was wondering when you'd contact me. You really shouldn't worry so much, Jack."

Jack spoke quickly. "That's not why I'm contacting you. We have another problem. Sethra's on her way."

I was surprised. "On her way? To me or you?"

He answered promptly. "To you. She's after Vince. I've heard from a source of mine that she found out he's still alive and wants to finish business."

I groaned in irritation. "What a witch."

Then there was the sound of growling. I turned to see werewolves in wolf form creeping up to me and growling viciously. There were about five of them. I knew I was in trouble, especially when I saw that a young woman stood behind them. She wore a long blue cape with a hood over her white hair. I knew who it was. "Sethra."

She smiled, attempting to seem innocent. "Hello, Ashura." She grinned when she saw the pumpkin. "Hello, Prince Jack."

Jack glared at her. "So you're Sethra."

I gave her a cold smile. "It's been quite some time since we last saw each other, hasn't it? I've heard you've been a bad little girl, Sethra."

She chuckled. "Is that what you heard? Well, I can tell you I've been an extra good girl. In fact, I'm so good I'm going to get a very special present for it." She gave me that dark smile I knew was hiding inside. "I'm going to get to be queen."

The werewolves pounced on me, but I pulled out my ebony wand and waved it, knocking them all aside with a gust of magic. Jack could only watch. "Ashura, be careful. Your magic will only do so much against werewolves."

I gripped my wand, carefully thinking over my situation. "I know this, Jack." Everyone did. It was like a game of roshambo. Witch or wizard beat vampire, vampire beat werewolf, and, unfortunately for me at the moment, werewolf beat wizard or witch.

Sethra smiled, clearly pleased to have the upper hand on me. "Where are your little assistants now, Ashura?" She turned with a cold chuckle. "Have fun, boys." With that, she left me to fight off her werewolves.

I found I was having difficulty fighting them all off alone. That didn't surprise me. Powerful wizard or not, I was still handicapped in this fight, physically and magically. I had assistants for a reason, specifically vampire ones.

As I fought them off, one werewolf managed to sneak up behind me and pounce. Before I knew it, I was thrown to the ground. Jack's pumpkin rolled away from me. I felt claws and started shooting magic all around, trying to protect myself, but it was little use. I suddenly felt teeth sink into my leg, and I cried out. I could just hear Jack's voice, but I couldn't make anything out and I couldn't see him.

Just then, I heard a voice loud and clear. "Get down, Ashura!" I covered my head with my arms as a burst of magic knocked the werewolves aside. I looked up, my hair on my face and covered in snow, my clothes torn and wet. There stood Rebecca in the doorway of the shop, with an old staff. The werewolves saw they were up against a powerful magic-using brownie, as well as noticed how the commotion seemed to be attracting the attention of nearby magical townsfolk, and they decided to be smart. They growled at us and ran off.

THE DARK EXISTENCE

I sighed in relief and lay on the ground, worn out and in pain. I looked to where the pumpkin was and sighed when I saw it had gotten smashed by Rebecca's spell. I hoped Jack wasn't too worried about me.

Rebecca hurried to my side. "You're not too hurt, are you?"

I shook my head. "One bit me, but nothing else to be concerned about."

Then I heard other voices. "Boss!" Oz and Sid ran over. They quickly helped me back into my wheelchair as Rebecca hurried inside to get something for the bite on my leg.

Oz looked worried. "I knew one of us should have stayed behind with you."

Sid spoke. "Are you okay, boss? What happened?"

I tried to ease their worry by speaking calmly. "Sethra showed up and left me a present. It was just a few werewolves, and Rebecca scared them off."

They still looked worried about me as Rebecca came outside and started taking a look at the bite.

Then Jason and Vince hurried over. Vince was carrying Tamarr as Jason led him along. I smiled when I saw Jason. "Oh, good, you're alive."

He looked at me in surprise. "What happened to you?"

I shook my head. "Nothing important. Just some werewolf trouble. I see you succeeded in getting the crown. Well done."

He nodded but still seemed concerned. "Yeah, though you weren't the only one who ran into werewolf trouble."

Vince groaned. "They said something when they showed up, something about cleaning up. What did they mean by that?"

I explained as Rebecca went inside for some bandages. "Sethra sent them to kill you, Vince. Jack said she found out you're alive and wants to finish what she started. To be honest, I don't think she even knows Jason is here or that he was after the Sorcerer's Crown."

Jason looked a bit relieved. "Then I may have an upper hand."

Then Rebecca came back outside and said, "Uh, your pumpkin friend is back."

I was expecting another pumpkin, but I was surprised when Jack himself walked out of the shop with her. He wore a long black velvet cape with orange fur lining, with a large hood over his head.

I smirked upon seeing him. "Of course, you'd worry."

He gave a smile of relief. "I see you're all, all right. I had begun to fear the worst."

He really was one of the kindest souls I knew. "Well, we're all fine."

Jack noticed Jason and smiled. "You have it."

Jason nodded as he touched the crown around his head. "Yeah, but you guys could have mentioned it doesn't come off."

I chuckled. "Well, now you know." I winced in pain as Rebecca used a healing spell to help me heal quicker.

Once she finished, she smiled sweetly. "You should be better soon."

I smiled back gratefully. "Thank you, Rebecca."

With that, she went back inside.

Jack spoke up once she left. "I'm afraid I have some other bad news. I just learned that Sethra's changed her plans. She's no longer waiting until Hallows' Eve night. She's moving out tonight." That wasn't good.

I ran a hand through my hair. "That wretched girl. No doubt something happened to make her plans even riskier. Probably trouble with her little troops."

Jason felt the jewel on the crown. "So what now?"

Jack looked concerned. "We have no choice but to face her now before her plans can even begin. I heard her troops started ahead, but she's staying back to prepare the spell. This gives us a good opening."

Vince looked worried. "But doesn't Jason need some kind of lesson on how not to be turned into a madman or something?"

I shook my head. "No time. It wouldn't matter anyway. It's only a matter of time and willpower now."

Jason had a look of slight worry, but he shook it away. "Then I'll go. Where can I find her?"

Jack was about to say something, probably to convince Jason not to rush into it, but I cut him off. "Her castle, I'm sure. It's not too far from here. Just head straight east, and you'll see it." Jack gave me a look, and I sighed. "It's too late to start doubting or rethinking this. He's got the crown. He needs to use it. If he's not quick, the entire surprise attack will fail, and we'll lose this precious opportunity you mentioned." I looked at him, becoming very serious. "He doesn't have time to waste here, Jack. This will all be for nothing if he doesn't go now. You know that."

Jack looked worried, knowing I was right. Jason smiled at him reassuringly. "I'll be fine." He started floating, which impressed me. He smiled. "This could actually be pretty easy."

Vince changed into vampire form since the sun was already out of sight, thanks to the shorter daylight time in the North, and he started flying. "Well, you're not going without me."

Jason raised an eyebrow. "You're blind."

He smirked. "That ever stop me before? I'll be fine. We're partners, man. We go in it together. Besides, knowing Sethra, she won't be alone. Fighting her will be trouble enough without extra players, so you'll need the extra help."

Jason sighed. "Oh, fine. Only because you're too stubborn, and I'm smart enough not to get into a fight I can't win."

Tamarr sighed. "Be careful, guys."

Jack looked upset. "I just wish I could come help you. At least that. You shouldn't have to go alone."

I spoke up. "You know you can't do that. Being the Pumpkin Prince and an original target of the first Sorcerer, you would only be a liability if Jason loses control. The fewer people go, the less friendly fire if that happens."

Jack clearly knew that, but it deeply pained him.

Jason smiled at him. "I'll be back soon. So don't worry, Oden."

That caught me by surprise. "Oden?"

I looked at Jack, and he looked astonished. With that, Jason and Vince flew off for Sethra's castle.

Of course, I knew Oden was Jack's middle name, but how did Jason know that? Why did it seem to mean so much to Jack that he did? As I looked at Jack, I could see the joy of hearing Jason say his middle name in his eyes, almost like it was familiar and comforting to him.

I immediately remembered something from a very long time ago. "Wait a minute! Don't tell me… Jason… he was…"

Jack only smiled as he remembered. I felt both happy for my friend and utterly mortified.

What had we done?

JASON

Vince flew at my side through the night air, toward the large castle on the side of the mountain. I felt courage rush through me as we reached the castle and landed outside it. Vince sighed. "So what's our battle plan?"

I had thought about that as we were flying. "We're here to stop Sethra from finishing that spell, right? Then that's what we'll do. We stop Sethra from finishing the spell, we stop her plans. Once her plans are stopped, she can give up, or we can somehow capture her."

Vince grinned. "Works for me. We just need to know where to find her and figure out just who all is here in the castle with her. She's really high-maintenance, so she's probably in some fancy bedroom making out with Jamal."

I glanced at him. "You really hate them, don't you?"

He scoffed. "Those lowlifes tried to kill me—*twice*! I *despise* them like nothing else in this or any other world!"

I grinned. "I guess that's as good a reason as any."

THE DARK EXISTENCE

We flew up along the castle, staying in the shadows cast by the full moon above. It was large in the starless sky, making the shadows seem so much darker. We stopped at a lone lit window near the top of the castle, and I peeked in.

Inside was a large beautiful bedroom fit for a queen. There were a few witches and werewolves there, as if keeping guard. Among them was the beautifully evil witch, Sethra, reading out a spell from a large ancient-looking book as she waved her staff in different patterns. She was clearly pretty focused on the spell.

I sighed and spoke softly. "Now what? Do we stand a chance against that many alone? And where's Jamal?"

Vince was listening closely. "Two werewolves and three witches, including Sethra, while maybe five vampires, two more werewolves, and about four wizards are somewhere on the floor below us. Honestly, this is not in our favor." He rubbed his chin. "Though if I'm right, I could change that."

I grinned. "How do you plan to do that?"

He grinned. "You just leave that to me, kid. When the time is right, go for it. Got it?" He started flying down the castle.

I spoke up. "How do I know when the time is right?"

He smiled. "You'll know it when you see it. Good luck."

With that, he flew down and snuck in through a window, out of sight. I sighed. "You too."

THE SILVER SPARROW

I went back to watching the room, waiting for what he was talking about. A few minutes went by before I heard a loud noise from the floor below. The witches inside the room left to check it out, but Sethra and the two werewolves stayed. I smirked. "Nice, Vince."

I then noticed a second window hidden behind some closed curtains. I flew to that window and eased it open silently. Lucky thing Sethra took care of her castle. Too bad it would be her undoing.

I thought of something and pulled on the hood of my coat so it hid my crown. I wanted to completely overwhelm her and take her by total surprise. Maybe it could give me the upper hand on her if she didn't know what she was really up against. Anything helped at this point. I slipped in and slid the window closed.

I could hear Sethra saying the spell out loud, though it sounded like a different language to me. I peeked out as she chuckled, waving her wand in circles as it flashed red and pink a couple of times. "Just a few more hours, and this will finally be over. The King of Night will wish he had never crossed me. I'll rip his crown right off his head and place it on my own. The very first Queen of Night. Oh, what a beautiful thought."

I saw the werewolves glance at each other, both clearly not interested in Sethra's little fantasy. I saw that the door was closed and had a lock on the inside. I concentrated on the lock, and it turned. I grinned.

THE DARK EXISTENCE

Couldn't have anyone getting in and ruining the surprise, could I?

Sethra must have sensed my magic, because she stopped fantasizing and doing the spell to look at the door. She looked around the room suspiciously. The werewolves seemed to notice her concern. They even noticed the door was locked.

Sethra looked that way again, giving me my chance. I stepped out from behind the curtain and grinned a dark grin like Ashura would. "Hello, Sethra."

She jumped and spun around. The werewolves were on their guard and started to growl. Sethra looked surprised, curious, and confused. I gave her a dark smile. "Remember me?"

She looked as if she was seeing a ghost. "That can't be. You're dead."

I chuckled darkly, acting just as dark and mysterious as Ashura. "Dead, huh? Last I remember, that was your fault, wasn't it?"

She looked caught between fear and rage. She was furious to know I wasn't dead, but she wasn't quite sure I wasn't. She managed to get some words out. "What are you doing here? *How* are you here?"

I chuckled and took a couple of steps forward, keeping up the dark act. "You tell me. Don't ghosts usually roam the earth because they have unfinished business to take care of?"

She took a step back from me, but then she toughened up and stepped forward. "You're no ghost. You don't look anything like a ghost." She pointed her long, thin staff at me. She grinned darkly. "I don't know how you survived or how you're here, but I'll be the one finishing business tonight."

She shot a ball of green light at me, but a magical green barrier, much like Ashura's, blocked it. She looked surprised, then grew angrier. She tried again and again, but it didn't do her any good.

I chuckled. "Okay, now it's my turn." I imagined a ball of red light in front of me, and it appeared, flying right at Sethra, who also created a barrier to block it.

She smirked. "I guess I'll just have to use more powerful magic to deal with you."

She glanced at the spell book, probably to make sure she didn't lose her place in the spell. I assumed that was the book her sisters had made such a big deal about, the one that showed her how to do that forbidden spell. From how she seemed to need to focus on the words in it while doing the spell, I had a feeling this had just become a little bit easier for me.

She fired a beam of light, and I put up a barrier again, except the beam knocked me and the barrier back into the wall painfully. I groaned and stood up. So there were some spells you couldn't simply block. No big deal.

She smirked. "I'm quite impressed. You must be a powerful wizard to withstand my power. How you tricked me into thinking you were a mortal before, I'll never know. No doubt this was Vince's plan from the very beginning. That would explain why you two aren't dead."

THE DARK EXISTENCE

She tried the beam again, but I dodged it. It blew a hole in the wall. I smirked. "Nice. You're destroying your own castle for me. Thanks."

She didn't appreciate that and shot at me again, but I dodged again. I tried a beam at the same time she did, and they collided in the middle. She grinned. "Oh, please. There's no way a brat like you could be more powerful than me."

I smirked darkly. "Wanna bet?"

My beam started to overpower hers. She was shocked as the beam hit her, knocking her into the back wall. The werewolves watched in surprise.

She glared at them. "Don't just stand there, you mangy wolves! Get him!"

They growled at her but turned to me.

I smirked. "Pushovers. Letting a silly little witch girl tell you what to do."

One scoffed. "It's not for her. It's for our prince. We will serve Prince Jamal loyally."

Prince? Jamal was a prince? That explained why the werewolves were so willing to do whatever Sethra said.

Just then, I felt the crown get warm. I gasped as I saw an image in my mind. It was someone with dark skin and long dark hair lying dead on the floor. I had never seen him before, but I knew just who it was.

I shook my head. "Jamal."

They crept up to me, ready to pounce.

I sighed. "There's no point since he's dead."

They stopped in shock. One growled at me. "What did you say?"

The other growled too. "What did you do to our leader?"

I scoffed. "I didn't do anything." I pointed at Sethra and continued, "If I had to guess, she did. She's done it before, killing Vince just because he was catching on to her real plans."

They looked back at her. She looked furious. No doubt she was ticked that I was trying to turn them against her. They saw it and growled at her. "Where is our leader, witch?"

She said, "No doubt with the others already. As I said before, he went to finish something for me before we started the invasion. He's just trying to fool you! I would never hurt my love!"

I could imagine that would happen. After all, from how Vince had described their relationship, Jamal would have done anything for her. They would have every reason to believe her over me. This was proven when they turned to me with snarling growls.

I groaned, but before I could say anything, I felt a strange pain in my head. Without even thinking it, I shot an enormous spell and blasted a hole in the wall where the door was, smashing the whole wall and door to pieces.

I was surprised. I didn't do that! It did that itself? Could this be the crown overpowering my will already?

THE DARK EXISTENCE

I groaned as I turned to Sethra. I needed to finish this now before the crown got any stronger. It was time to ruin Sethra's day.

She shot another spell at me, which I ducked from before throwing a ball of fire at her. Though when she dodged it, I used the crown to make it change direction.

Sethra saw where the spell was headed, and she gasped in horror. "*No!*"

She couldn't do anything in time as the fire hit her book, and it burst into flames. She went to put it out, but I shot her away from it, preventing her from saving the book from its fiery end.

Sethra was horrified. "No... the book of black magic..." She glared at me, enraged. "You little—! You have no idea what you have just called on yourself!"

She created a flash of light that blinded me for a moment, then shot me with a powerful blast that sent me flying out the room, right into the open air outside. I managed to shake off the daze and start flying, only for me to look up and gasp. There was Sethra, flying after me on her broomstick, her staff now aimed at me. "I'll kill you for this, brat!"

I flew from her, dodging her powerful spells. We flew all around the castle in the moonlight, shooting spells at each other. Suddenly, a sneak attack caught me off guard and knocked me into the castle, crashing through a large window. I groaned as I sat up. I was in a big empty room, like an undecorated ballroom.

Sethra flew in with an evil smile. "End of the line, boy."

I smirked. "You'd think so, wouldn't you?"

Just then, a few witches, wizards, and werewolves rushed in, though they weren't coming after me. In fact, they were busy fighting. That's when I saw Vince and the five vampires he mentioned, all fighting the others.

I smirked. So Vince had managed to convince the vampires to side with us, giving him some allies to keep the other night creatures working for Sethra busy. From how the werewolves, witches, and wizards were going down and staying down, it looked like the vampires were winning.

Sethra stepped off her broom and faced me. "You haven't beaten me yet! This may not have gone the way I had hoped, but I can find another spell book and start over again by Hallows' Eve!" She noticed the now unconscious werewolves. "And now thanks to this attack, the others will believe me when I tell them it was you who killed Jamal! That it was Vince who went traitor and helped you slaughter him in the name of the King of Night! His werewolves will have no trouble believing me, and once you're all dead, I'll—"

She suddenly stopped with a gasp when her eyes finally fell on my forehead, which was no longer hidden by my hood because she had sort of shot it off while we were in the air. She looked horrified.

I grinned. "Still think it's the end of the line for me?"

THE DARK EXISTENCE

She spoke softly. "So that's how you did it. You were a mortal, still are, but you've gotten the Sorcerer's Crown."

The night creatures, including the vampires, gasped and backed away from me.

I grinned. "That would be wise."

I felt the crown start to hurt my head again. I shot a spell at the last two witches, but they dodged just in time. I shot a few more, causing everyone to have to duck and dodge, including Vince and the vampires with him.

I felt myself grin. "I will not lose to some pathetic little witch and her toy army. I have more than enough power to wipe you all out in one shot!" I found it hard to make my body do what I wanted. I feared I was right. The crown was taking control of me.

Sethra could see it in my eyes, and she looked afraid. "What have you done, fool?"

I laughed quite insanely. "You really think a worthless little girl like you will get to be ruler of the Hallows Realm? Ha! The King of Night's crown rightfully belongs to me!" I gave her an evil grin that terrified her. "If you really want that crown, then I guess you'll just have to be the first to go."

She looked like her legs were going to give out on her any minute. They actually did give out as I started toward her. Everyone was terrified of me. I couldn't let myself lose to this stupid crown.

I stopped and held my head, trying to clear out the awful thoughts that were trying to control it.

Sethra saw my moment of weakness and took advantage of it. She grabbed one of the werewolves' swords and charged at me. Just before she reached me, someone jumped in the way. The sword ran him through, and I felt myself suddenly have a burst of willpower. "Vince!"

Vince collapsed to his knees, holding the hilt of the sword protruding from his gut. I went down beside him. "Vince! Vince, are you okay?"

He grabbed the hilt and pulled it out with a cry. He tossed it away and held the area where he was stabbed. I saw blood run from the corner of his mouth. I felt my heart beat fast.

Before I could do anything to help him, Sethra shot me with a spell. I was knocked back across the floor. I saw her about to shoot Vince, but I jumped to my feet and slammed into her. She hit the floor painfully, but she wasn't beaten. She glared at me. "Get him!"

The wizards who were still on their feet took advantage of the vampires' surprise to create vines from the ground that caught the vampires and stalled them as they came to challenge me. I felt power build up inside me, so I let it out. I released a blast of powerful magic, sending them, and even a few of the vampires who got free, right into the wall, which now had an enormous hole.

Sethra looked worried, but her rage was stronger. She started shooting at me with spells. I knocked them aside with a flash of light. I glanced at Vince. He was bleeding heavily and lying on the floor, on his side. He was clearly not going to heal like last time, so I knew I had to do something, and fast.

I shot another enormous blast at Sethra, just to distract her, and ran to Vince's side. I went down beside him and saw a shard of glass on the floor. I grabbed it to cut my hand, but he grabbed my wrist, stopping me. He groaned weakly. "We really need to stop this habit. The more of your blood I drink, the more I'll want. Trust me, the last thing you want is a vampire getting a taste for your blood."

I opened my mouth to say that I couldn't just leave him like that, but someone quickly flew over.

I was surprised to find it was Oz. He grinned. "Sorry we got here a little late, but we figured better late than never, right?"

I noticed Sid nearby, helping the other vampires fight off the last wizard and witch. Oz pulled out a vial and helped Vince drink it as I created a barrier to protect us from Sethra's attacks.

Vince groaned as he seemed to already be slowly recovering. "You carry human blood on you, Oz? Aren't you part phantom?"

Oz looked surprised. "How'd you figure that out?"

Vince smirked. "You haven't made a single sound since we first met you, except when you talk. I happen to know a phantom personally, so I easily noticed how similar you seemed to him, especially with how much I rely on sound now."

Oz cleared his throat. "Yeah, well, it's actually Sid's. I don't drink blood. Can't, really."

I watched them. "So you'll be okay, Vince?"

He nodded. "Yeah, I'll recover now. Just, you know, try not to get yourself killed, okay? I don't think I can take another blow for you like that."

I let Oz help Vince get back up as I stood up and faced Sethra. She laughed. "So that's how Vince is still alive. You gave him some of your blood, didn't you? I guess he didn't drink enough of your blood to kill you, so you repaid the favor. Now it makes sense."

I glared at her. "You're gonna regret trying to kill him a third time, witch."

She grinned. "Oh, you wish. Once I'm through with you, I'll make sure his death is slow and painful. I'll make sure of it myself this time."

That was more than enough for me.

We threw magic around like the food fights back home at my school, ducking and dodging each other's spells. Some spells missed; some hit. It was an all-out war between us. Over and over, the crown managed to get the better of me and nearly hurt the others.

Luckily, none hurt Vince, whom Oz and Sid did their best to keep out of harm's way, though he still held his wound. He was still bleeding, but not nearly as much as before, clearly healing a lot slower than back at Convile's castle.

Once again, I lost control and shot a spell that knocked Sethra to the floor painfully. She had a hard time getting up this time. I laughed maniacally. "Quit wasting my time! Don't you ever just give up?"

THE DARK EXISTENCE

She glared up at me. "Not a chance. Not when I'm about to win." She smirked. "I wonder how well that other spell from my book will work on someone wearing the Sorcerer's Crown."

Suddenly, I felt a horrible pain in my head. I held my head and cried out. It was like a siren was going off in my brain. I fell to my knees, squeezing my head tightly, mentally begging it to stop.

She laughed. "Seems it works like a charm! Good thing I managed to memorize some of the other ancient curses before you destroyed my spell book. This specific curse will cause your power to rise to a horribly painful level that will hurt you more than ever before."

I felt like my head was going to explode, and breathing became so much harder to do. I fell to my side, still gripping my head.

Sethra stood over me. "It's over, brat." She held her staff over me, and it started to glow a bright deadly green. She grinned. "Goodbye."

Just as the spell was about to finish me, something suddenly slammed into her. The horrible pain subsided, and I lay limp on the ground. Vince managed to reach me, ignoring his injury. "Kid, you okay?"

I managed a few weak words. "I can't move."

He smiled softly. "That's no surprise. After a curse like that, you're lucky you're even still alive."

I heard Sethra gasp. I managed to turn my head and was equally surprised. There stood a familiar figure facing her now. However, what surprised me was that the one time I had seen this figure, he had been lying dead on the floor somewhere.

Sethra was shocked. "J-Jamal?"

Jamal, now an incredibly good-looking guy, glared at her with a powerful hatred, and even a bit of hurt, in his eyes. "Hello, Sethra." Even his voice was smooth as honey, perfectly matching his good looks. No wonder people thought werewolves were incredibly handsome.

Just then, a whole pack of werewolves in different forms rushed into the room, surrounding Sethra, Vince, and me. Vince stayed close to me, protecting me from them, even though we both knew he couldn't do anything.

Sethra still spoke very softly, unsure what to make of the figure she was so sure she had killed. "But you're dead."

Jamal's voice was cold and blunt. "I promised I'd haunt you, didn't I?"

She noticed the werewolves growling as they closed in a bit. She held out her staff to protect herself. "Stay back! Or I'll kill you all!"

The werewolves stopped closing in, but they weren't backing off.

Jamal spoke angrily. "I should have known better than to trust a witch like you, Sethra. You used me, you betrayed me, and now I have no choice but to stop you from destroying everything."

That's when another voice spoke up. "Not that it will be hard."

THE DARK EXISTENCE

I looked to see a new wizard walk over, the werewolves stepping aside to let him through. What grabbed my attention right away was his strange glowing golden eye.

He spoke with a cold smile. "Thanks to this mortal, I had more than enough time to save Jamal and show him to the rest of your little army as proof of just what kind of witch you really are. They easily believed us and have already disbanded. Your army is no more, Sethra."

Sethra was horrified. "No! But... why? Flynn, you want the king dead just as much as I do! Why would you do this?"

Flynn sighed. "Because this isn't how I want it to go. You and I both know what you were doing wasn't going to help the realm. What's the point of killing the king if it will just make everything for the realm worse? Quite frankly, I was against this whole thing before I even agreed to help you with it. I simply played along so I could make sure you failed."

He continued in a scoffing tone, "Plus, I was in no way willing to trust a stupid little witch like you with such a powerful and ancient book of black magic. I knew I just needed to get it away from you before you could do the spell, but how could I do that with so many night creatures around all the time to stop me?"

He smirked. "Jason created the perfect diversion and even managed to destroy the book. So that was two birds with one stone, while I took care of the rest." He glanced down at me with a smirk. "So for that, you have my thanks, mortal." I was too weak to even care.

Sethra glared at them. "You won't get away with this. None of you! I'll make you all pay!"

Flynn smirked as his eye began to glow brighter. "Oh? Well, we can't have that now, can we, Jamal?" Sethra was surprised as her staff suddenly flew from her hand and into Flynn's. He smirked as he snapped it in two. "If you really are that dedicated to getting revenge and finding a way to try something like this again, then we have no choice but to make sure you never can."

Sethra looked genuinely frightened now, making me actually feel for her a little as she looked at Jamal. "J-Jamal? You… You wouldn't kill me. Not me. You… You love me, don't you? You need me!"

Jamal's face was hard and cold. "How did you put it?" He glared at her. "Oh, right. 'I don't need you. I never did.' Isn't that right?"

Sethra was horrified, but she clearly had nothing she could say against that.

He turned from her. "I can't have you getting in my way, Sethra. Love doesn't replace the safety of my kind or the realm they call home." He glanced back at her, no sign of love in his eyes whatsoever. "I will be the future king my kind needs me to be. Clearly, I can't be that with someone like you distracting me."

She looked afraid but didn't budge.

Jamal spoke softly. "Goodbye, 'my love.'"

THE DARK EXISTENCE

Vince turned my face away from them as the werewolves lowered themselves. "Trust me, you don't wanna see this part."

I was honestly glad he did that as I heard them pounce and Sethra let out a bloodcurdling scream. The sounds I heard as they tore her apart sent shivers down my spine and made my blood run cold. I didn't dare look back.

Then I heard footsteps come in my direction. Vince leaned over me and blocked the way with his one arm. He hissed, "You stay away from him, Jamal." The steps stopped as he continued. "You may have killed Sethra, but I still don't trust you!"

I heard Jamal speak. "Why should it matter? Once the King of Night finds out, he'll be dead anyway. I would be doing him a favor killing him quickly, rather than letting the King of Night kill him slowly and mercilessly."

Vince hissed, "Because if you wanna lay a finger on him, you go through me first, pup! I've been protecting this kid way too much to let you show up and kill him now!"

Jamal scoffed. "Then what, Vince? He's wearing the Sorcerer's Crown! Either someone kills him, or he'll kill all of us! You think Sethra was dangerous? You should see what he will be capable of once the crown takes control! He could barely control it fighting Sethra on his first day wearing it. What makes you think he'll handle it after this? It will slowly take his will and turn him into the monster the Sorcerer once was!"

THE SILVER SPARROW

Vince was silent a moment, then he said, "Your father would have given him a chance."

Even I could tell that was a low blow as I heard Jamal's quick intake of breath, then his low growl. "What would you know about my father, you stupid bat?"

Vince scoffed. "That's a stupid question, and you know it. You and I may not have worked together with Sethra long, but you know enough about me from before that to know I have every right to say it." He glared in Jamal's direction. "After all, you wouldn't even be here if not for your father being so forgiving. Especially when your mother came along."

Jamal growled. "All right, I get it! Shut up!" He growled, not saying a word for a moment.

It was Flynn who spoke up. "Come on, Jamal. We're done here."

Jamal finally spoke. "Very well. I won't touch him. However, don't be surprised when the King of Night is not nearly so forgiving, Vince. This kid is your problem now, and I hope you realize that every life he takes will be on your head."

Vince smirked. "That's a risk I'm willing to take for him."

I couldn't help but smile to see how confident he was in me.

Then I heard Jamal walk away. "Let's go, werewolves."

I looked to see them all walking away, now all in wolf form. As Jamal reached the door with Flynn, I noticed Flynn say something I couldn't hear to him.

THE DARK EXISTENCE

I could hear the werewolves' padded paws walking away. It sounded a lot like rain. I felt my eyelids grow heavy and my body grow weak.

Vince said, "Jason? Jason, are you okay? Why is your light going out? Jason?"

I couldn't answer him. Everything was getting dark, and my body was getting sleepy. I heard Vince say my name a couple more times and even just caught the sound of Oz and Sid's voices before I finally let go and everything went black.

JASON

I woke up with a start, sitting up fast—too fast. I became light-headed and groaned. Then I heard a familiar voice say, "You're awake."

I looked and was surprised to see I was in the living room of the Phantom Mansion. I saw Vince sitting in an armchair that had been pulled up beside the couch. He smiled. "You okay, Jason?"

I looked around. "We're in the Phantom Mansion. How?"

He chuckled. "Yeah, you can thank Michael for that. Can you believe it? He helped me, Oz, and Sid get out of Sethra's castle and back here without any trouble from the other werewolves. Apparently, he's Jamal's apprentice and had come to help Jamal at the castle. That's when he saw us. Kid felt awfully guilty, so he helped us out and managed to heal you up."

He shrugged. "Seems he's the reason Sethra knew I was alive. He told Jamal about everything we had told Fen and the others here. Though that was before Sethra tried to kill Jamal, and somehow she didn't know everything else we were doing. Guess I was the only thing Jamal managed to tell her before she 'killed' him."

THE DARK EXISTENCE

I sighed. "Sethra's dead. Does that mean we won?"

Vince laughed. "Yep, we won."

I smiled. "That's good."

I felt my head and found the crown was still there. Vince seemed to hear my hand move to my head. "Headache or crown?"

I smirked. "You're really getting the hang of being blind. To answer your question, crown."

He sighed. "Ashura said you are the most incredible person he's ever met in all his life. And trust me, based on how old he really is, that's a *very* long time."

I laughed. "That's some seriously high praise coming from him, I'm sure."

Vince leaned back in the chair with a smile. "So how do you feel?"

I shrugged. "Myself. I have my own free will, if that's what you're asking."

He chuckled.

Then Veil and some others came into the house. She saw me and smiled sweetly. "Oh, good. You're awake." She hurried over and sat on the edge of the couch, beside me. "How do you feel, dear?"

I smiled as Fen, Michael, Ashura, Oz, and Sid came over too. "I'm fine."

Ashura watched me with a kind smile, his wheelchair being pushed by Sid. "Welcome back, Jason."

I chuckled. "Thanks. I hear I've really impressed you."

He nodded as he leaned back in his chair. "Well, you're the first person to survive the Sorcerer's Crown,

THE SILVER SPARROW

so it would be rather silly of me not to give that a lot of credit. And more than that, you just saved the Hallows Realm and the mortal realm while using the crown that should have taken control over your very soul. From everything Vince, Oz, and Sid told me about it, I can see your will is connected to how you feel."

I thought back to what happened. "That makes sense. I managed to get control every time I saw Vince. He was already hurt because of me, and I didn't want anything else to happen to him, especially not by my hand."

Ashura smiled understandingly. "That's good. It just means it won't bother you if you just remember what matters most to you." I gasped, and he noticed. "What?"

I remembered Jack making me promise to remember—to remember what was most important. That was what he meant. That was how he helped me know how to use the crown right. I had to remember what was most important to me to make my willpower strong enough to overpower the crown.

I smiled. "Seems Jack taught me how to use the crown after all."

"Someone mention my name?"

We all looked to see Jack walk over, wearing a royal black cape with orange trimming and his symbol on the back. It was the same symbol from his banners, the pumpkin and the scythe. He even wore a gold circlet shaped like vines intertwining around his head. Everyone moved aside with polite bows and curtsies so he could stand beside the couch.

Tamarr hopped off Jack's shoulder onto my lap. "Glad to see you're up, kid."

I rubbed behind his ear. "Thanks, Tamarr. Glad to see you too. For a moment there, I thought I'd never see any of you again."

They all smiled at me.

Then I noticed Michael staring at the floor off to one side, so I spoke up. "Hey, Michael."

He looked at me, clearly ashamed.

I simply smiled at him. "Thanks for your help."

He looked a bit surprised, then nodded. "Sure." He managed a little smile. "Hope it makes up for opening my big mouth in the first place. Jamal's my mentor and my leader, so I felt obligated to tell him."

I could understand. "Hey, I can respect that. You did what you thought you should. That's sorta how this realm works now with this lousy unbalance. Not your fault."

Jack smiled kindly, knowing I was referring to him too.

I turned to him with a grin. "So. Oden Lantern."

Everyone but Ashura was surprised. Jack chuckled. "I see you got your memory back."

I nodded. "Also seems you never lost yours."

He sat where Veil had been sitting a minute ago. "I guess I honestly couldn't bear to forget. Besides, now I see it was a good thing I didn't." He smiled at me, reminding me of the person I once looked up to as my best friend. "It's still so hard to believe it's really

THE SILVER SPARROW

you. It wasn't until I saw your courage the first time, back when I was trying to make you give up on the Sorcerer's Crown, that I realized it really was you."

I smirked. "So you did cause that. That courage thing I keep getting. You gave me that at the pool."

He smiled as he thought back. "Yes, I did. You just looked so scared. I wanted to give you a little help. So I gave you a spell that doubles your feelings of courage. Once you start to feel courageous, it will be twice as strong."

That explained so much. "That's pretty cool and explains a lot. I used to have trouble being afraid of anything growing up. My mom used to worry it was because I was hit by that truck." I turned to him with an annoyed look. "Dude, you let me get hit by a truck."

Jack laughed. "No, you were never hit by a truck. I just made it look like you were. Gave you a few touches that made you look like you were seriously injured, though you never felt a thing. In fact, I bet when you woke up in the hospital, you were in no pain, like it never happened."

I thought about it and grinned. "Now that I think about it, yeah. I never felt anything. The doctors all said it was because I had healed before I woke up, but I guess it was never there to begin with."

Jack smiled. "Nope. I said it before. I would never let anything happen to you."

I sighed and said with a smile, "Too bad my mom didn't know that before she passed. Might have eased her mind a bit."

THE DARK EXISTENCE

He looked at me kindly. "Your mother's no longer with you?"

I shook my head. "No, she passed away three years ago."

Jack looked sympathetic as he remembered. "I'm sorry to hear that. She was a very kind woman. Always reminds me of Veil here." Veil smiled. I had to agree. They were a lot alike, though my mom had brown hair and blue eyes, and wasn't nearly as tall.

Then others walked in. It was the Witching Sisters and Melody. Melody saw me and smiled, blushing a bit. I smiled back. "Hi, ladies." Of course, Berleen and Leanndra hurried over, fangirling over me.

Jack sighed and said with a smile, "Well, I'm glad you're better, Jason." He stood up and looked down at me. "Come by the castle when you're fully recovered, okay?"

I nodded. "Sure thing."

He headed for the door, but then he stopped. "Oh, by the way," he said, turning back to me with a smile, "happy Halloween, Jason."

Jack-O'-Lantern

I watched the mirror before me show my memories as Oden Lantern. I was sitting on my pedestal, watching my mirror with a smile. I saw Jason in it, standing by the pool, too afraid to get in. I smiled as I watched the spell of courage rush through him, and he finally climbed in, giving me that proud smile of his. I chuckled just as someone walked in. I turned to them as my mirror returned to showing me my reflection.

Jason and Vince stood before the platform. Tamarr hopped off of Jason's shoulder and hopped up onto my lap. I rubbed behind his ears as I spoke. "Feeling better, Jason?"

He nodded, letting the light glint off the Sorcerer's Crown. Though I guess it should be called Jason's crown now. After all, he was permanently stuck with it. Jason said, "So what now, Jack?"

I looked at him. "What do you mean?"

He smirked. "Well, I've got a crazy powerful crown stuck to my head, and I'm in a realm where witches and werewolves try to kill me."

He really hadn't changed much from that kid I knew. "My, you've had quite the adventure. That

THE DARK EXISTENCE

deserves a good rest in your own world, with your family."

Jason scoffed. "Yeah, my family. My little brother who's probably happily stuffing his face with candy at my aunt's house and my dad who won't be home till Christmas. Since Mom died, the guy's never home." He then groaned and said with an annoyed smile, "And I totally missed getting a buttload of candy last night."

We all laughed. Of course, I knew what Hallows' Eve was now in the mortal realm.

I smiled as I continued to scratch behind Tamarr's ear. "And it's thanks to you anyone got to enjoy the night at all. After all, you're the one who stopped the invasion that was supposed to have taken place last night. All those little candy-eaters are in your debt, as are we."

Jason smiled and scratched behind his head, embarrassed by the high praise. "Thanks, Jack."

Vince nudged him and said with a grin, "Well, don't feel bad, kid. You'll still have me hanging around."

Jason seemed a bit surprised. "Really? You're coming back with me?"

Vince nodded. "You bet! What, were you hoping I wouldn't? Still scared of the big mean vampire hanging out at your school?"

Jason thought about it. "But what about the Fawx family? Won't they miss you if you leave again?"

Vince shrugged. "Yeah, but I can always visit. And besides, you still need me, and I need you. We're partners."

Jason smiled. "Yeah, partners."

They sealed the deal as they shook hands.

I was glad to see it. "Seems you two have become rather close companions."

Jason smiled. "Yeah. When you continue to save each other's lives, you can't really help it."

A very true point, one I had watched come true time and time again. "Well, then I do hope you both take care in the mortal realm. And remember, Jason, you shouldn't use the crown for any reason. Using it will cause it to try to control you. It won't bother you if you don't wake it up. And try to control your feelings. Strong negative emotions could awaken it if you're not careful."

Jason nodded. "Yeah, Ashura explained everything last night. I'll be fine."

Strangely enough, I believed him. "I'm sure you will be."

Then he thought of something. "One question though. When you came to the mortal realm before, you said your dad had made a mistake, and you were trying to fix it. Something about finding someone. I can assume you were serious about that."

I sighed and nodded. I had feared this would come.

He continued, "Whatever did happen to that guy? You left so suddenly, I wasn't sure if you ever got him."

THE DARK EXISTENCE

Vince was curious. "Why'd you leave suddenly?"

I explained patiently, "I left because that was when my father refused to give up his crown. In fact, it was Tamarr here who called me the night before I left. He told me what my father had done, and because of that, I had to leave right away."

Jason seemed to understand. "So that's it." He then looked up at me and asked, "Did you ever get the guy you were looking for?"

I was hesitant, but I smiled. "Yes, I did." I felt Tamarr's claws on my leg, but I ignored it. "I found him."

Jason looked relieved. "That's good."

Vince smiled and nudged him. "Come on, man. Let's go. Your brother's probably a day away from calling the cops on you."

Jason smiled at me. "See you, Jack. Hopefully someday soon."

I smiled back. "Likewise."

I watched them leave, leaving Tamarr with me alone in the room.

Tamarr spoke once they were gone. "You shouldn't have lied to the kid."

I sighed, knowing he was right. "He's been through enough. Besides, I'm sure now it wasn't him."

He stood up. "But maybe he knows where we could find him. He could know where Arazon is. You did say you knew for sure he was there."

I shook my head. "I don't want to drag him into any more of this. He's done more than enough for now. I'll find Arazon myself soon enough."

He watched me with serious eyes, reminding me of the vampire he once was. "Yeah, but what if then it's too late?"

I looked at myself in the mirror. I saw myself as Oden Lantern. I could only shake my head. "I don't know."

Tamarr simply lay on my lap, no longer interested in discussing the matter. I looked at a pumpkin growing on the floor. It was old and starting to rot. Soon it would die.

I sighed sadly. "I fear our lives are in fate's hands now."

The End
…for now.

About the Author

The Silver Sparrow, known by name as Lydia Booker, is a young woman from little Pennsylvania living with her mother and five younger siblings. While her hobbies include playing computer games, reading, admiring nature through photography, listening to music, and swimming, none have ever compared to telling a good story.

Growing up, books of magical new people and places were Lydia's escape from a rough childhood. When she was twelve, she began writing her own books, finding inspiration in one day bringing smiles to others the way her favorite authors brought smiles to her darkest days. She's been writing and bringing smiles ever since.

Inspired by her love for Halloween, she was determined to make *The Dark Existence* a story that would have mystified her in her youth, a standard for every book she writes. After fifteen years of writing, perfecting, and getting lots of rejections, one of her earliest novels is now the first to ever be published.

CPSIA information can be obtained
at www.ICGtesting.com
Printed in the USA
BVHW032230090422
633897BV00005B/122

9 781638 817970